Unbroken

By Jennifer Neugin

Based on True Events

I want to thank my husband for getting us through all the ups and downs. If it weren't for your goodness, I wouldn't be here. For you, my first and always love.

<u>Table of Contents</u>

Preface

Death.

The word sends chills down our spines. It's a dark, frightening word. The thought of leaving this mortal coil is one fear that everyone shares. Some fear death because they don't know what's next. Is there a next? What's next? Where will I go? Others fear death because they don't know what will happen to the people that depend on them. They weren't ready to go. There was so much more to do, to say.

Some people don't have to grapple with the fear; they are taken home before they know what's going on. Then there are some that have time to make plans. They have time to face their fears and do the things they want to do, the things they need to do and say the things that need to be said. It's times like that which test a person's strength and faith.

Faith.

It almost sounds magical. It's not magic, but a well of strength given to us by the knowledge that God is there to guide us. He's the one that will never forsake you as long you don't want to be forsaken. He's there during the good times, celebrating with you, and he's there when the world seems the darkest. I know because he's always been there for me.

When they brought me into the hospital, my life was flashing before my eyes. I saw things I hadn't even thought of in years. Some of them were good memories, but there were so many I wish wouldn't have come up. It's easier to live with things when you're ignorant of them. Lying here, wondering if I will survive this latest illness, gives me time to think about what I saw when I was dying. It has given me the strength I need to put my story out there and give purpose to everything I've suffered.

1

"Go outside and play!"

"It's cold," I said, trying to go back in the warm house.

"You can't." She pushed me back out, "I've got a friend coming over, and we can't visit if you're around. GO! PLAY!"

Mom slammed the door in my face. Followed by the scraping of the lock. It wasn't usual for her to kick me out after my sister went to school. Mom seemed to have company every day. All were men. When they came, I would hide in the bushes, curious to see their faces. I never recognized any of them. It wasn't until I got older that I realized there was something wrong with that.

At first, when Mom sent me outside, I would stay in the

bushes. The world was big and scary to me. I was barely beyond the age of a toddler. I didn't want to get lost. So, I would sit there watching animals play, cars drive by, and listen for the man to leave. Then one day, the neighbor across the street saw me heading for my favorite spot in the bushes.

She called from the street.

"Little girl, what are you doing?"

I stared at her for a moment. I thought I was in trouble. A tear streaked down my cheek. If I wasn't supposed to be there, where was I supposed to go? What was I supposed to do?

She came closer, with a gnarled hand stretched out, "Come here, little girl. I'm not going to hurt you."

Looking from her hand to her nearly black eyes, I knew it would be okay to go with her. She had kind, wizened eyes. I knew I would be safer with her than with my mother. So I gave her my hand, and we headed to her house.

"What's your name, little girl?"

"Astrid."

"Astrid?"

I nodded while taking in the strange look of the street from the other side. The strangeness scared me at first. I wanted to go back to the bushes where I was hidden, where I knew I was safe. Then Nannie squeezed my hand, and the fear melted away. I was safe.

"Who are you?"

She smiled, "You can call me Nannie."

She led me into the house and sat me on the couch. With a sigh, she wrapped an afghan around me that smelled like roses. The scent relaxed me more. There was no tension there. After a couple of minutes at Nannie's house, I felt more comfortable then I ever had at home.

"Where are your shoes, Astrid?"

The question made me tense. "In my room," I whispered.

"Why didn't you put them on before you went outside?"

I stared at her, trying to hide in the blanket.

"Mommy just grabbed me and told me to get outside."

"Why?"

"She has a friend coming over, and she doesn't like me to be there."

Disgust sparked in her deep, dark eyes.

"Well, you don't have to hide anymore. Whenever your mommy sends you outside, you can come over here and keep me company."

I emerge further from the blanket. "OK."

"You hungry?"

I nodded. My stomach rumbled at the thought of food. Nannie must have heard it too, because she got a hard look on her face before she headed to the kitchen. In minutes, she had milk and eggs on the table.

She watched me eat eagerly with a strange look on her face. It wasn't until I was older that I realized the look was pity. It was a look I would see throughout my life from family, friends and the mirror. Nannie, however, was the first to pity me.

"Do you go to church?"

"Yes," I replied around the eggs in my mouth.

"What do you know about Jesus Christ?"

I shrugged, still more concerned with food.

"Let me tell you about him."
She got up and went to the
bookcase across the room.

From that day on, whenever Mom
kicked me out. I would go to
Nannie's. She would make me
cookies and read to me from the
Bible. When I was with Nannie, I
always felt loved and like I was
worth something. I felt like a
miracle of God instead of my
mother's punishment. In the short
time she was in my life, she was
my teacher, friend, and my true
mother. If it were not for her
Bible teachings, I don't know if
I would've had the strength to
endure the challenges that lay
ahead.

"ASTRID!"

"ASTRID!!"

Nannie pulled back the
curtains, a look of wonderment on
her face.

"Your mother is calling for you
Astrid. You better get home
before she tans your hide."

My fingers touched my swollen
lip, and I jumped off the couch
running full speed to the door.
Nannie opened it for me, and I
continued to my house. My mother
scowled at me as she watched me
leave Nannie's house.

"What the hell are you doing over there? Don't bother the neighbors. They don't want to deal with you any more than I do."

She smacked the back of my head as I came by, nearly sending me face-first into the grass.

"I'm sorry about that Mrs. Barton. I'll make sure she doesn't bother you anymore."

"She's not a bother to me. She's a very nice girl."

"I'm glad you think so, ma'am." She turned around, glaring at me with passionate hate. "Get your ass in the house."

Sitting on our couch was the man who had been visiting mom lately. He was dark-skinned like Nannie, but the same age as my mom. He looked nice until he smiled. There was something in his smile that scared me more than wandering the world by myself. It reminded me of the serpent from the story of Adam and Eve.

He took a couple of steps toward me, "Hi, there! What is your name?"

"Astrid. What is yours?"

"I'm John." He held out his hand.

Nannie taught me always to be polite, so I took it. "Nice to meet you."

"Your mommy has told me so much about you and your sister. I feel like I know you already." His smile seemed to grow darker the longer he spoke.

I looked at my mother, but she seemed only to have eyes for John.

"Can I play in my room," I asked.

Having broken the spell, she glared at me again. "Yes. Go away. John's staying for dinner, so I'll call you when it's ready."

It was interesting watching my mom around John. She laughed at everything he said and waited on him hand and foot. Even my sister Grace thought it was odd. She said Mom didn't act like that around Daddy. I had to take her word for it; I hardly remembered anything about Daddy. He'd been deployed overseas most of my life.

After dinner, my sister and I got cleaned up and ready for bed. Mom tucked my sister in and told her goodnight. She never did it with me. Every night she came by my room to make sure I'm there and turned off the light. I dropped off to sleep not long after saying the prayer Nannie taught me.

What happened that night is still a mystery to me, but it wasn't good. Sometime during the night, John came into my room. He shut and locked the door behind him. As he approached me, he started undressing. That night was the start of a new normal for me, for a while.

Nannie must have known something wasn't right because the way she taught the Bible changed. She didn't tell as many stories. It was more like memorizing different scriptures. She reminded me constantly that God never gives anyone more than they can handle. So the more arduous the trial seems, the more strength God knows someone has. Nannie always told me how much she loved me and how special I was.

My twisted version of normal shattered when I was about four, and Daddy came home from Vietnam. He picked up me and my sister from the babysitter. The babysitter our mother found made my mother's increasingly abusive behavior look like a walk in the park. Between the two, I always had bruises, abrasions, and the odd broken bone. Seeing Daddy gave me a sense of hope for the future. Hope for a real family, a happy family. The smile on his face gave me hope there was someone else in the world that loved me besides Nannie.

The day started out great; we were going to get pop. When you're little, pop is an amazing treat. I got a Big Red because I liked the color. Daddy asked all about us and told funny stories about when he was a kid. I smiled and laughed so much in the back seat, my face hurt.

It wasn't until my sister Grace got quiet that I realized something was wrong. We drove by the house and Mom's car was gone. She was off work that day. Tension filled the car like lava. Daddy looked like he was ready to burst.

"Where's your Mom?"

Grace and I looked at each other with the same fearful, uncertain expression. I truly didn't know where Mom was, but Grace did. Her face flushed, and her bottom lip quivered. Even though we weren't close, I wanted to comfort her as best I could.

Taking her hand, I squeezed it encouragingly.

He said, "You can tell me, I won't be mad." Then he would give this tight half smile that scared us.

Eventually, Grace broke and told Daddy where to find Mom. With a quiet "okay," he started the car. We ended up at the motel she was holed up in with John. He told us to stay in the car and stay down; he would be back. The look on his face brooked no argument from either of us. He went away for a few minutes and then stopped by the car, pulling something out of the trunk. Then we heard a loud crack.

I grabbed Grace, holding onto her tightly. She held onto me just as tightly. After a few minutes of yelling, we worked up enough courage to look out the passenger side window. Daddy had broken down the door one room over from where we had parked and found Mom in bed with John. Mom was crying, and Daddy was crying, but John was crying the hardest because Daddy had a shotgun in his mouth.

Daddy called John every nasty thing he could remember. Whenever Daddy couldn't talk, he would jab the gun farther into John's mouth, making him gag and cry harder. Mom kept begging Daddy to stop and not to hurt him. She apologized and tried explaining how they had grown apart. She blamed the stress of the war and having two kids, especially one like me. Daddy wasn't having any of it and told her to get the hell out of his house. At first, I was excited, thinking Grace and I would be staying with Daddy, but I wouldn't get that lucky.

Mom's Dad came from Illinois to take us all back with him. I cried uncontrollably. Mom told me to shut up, that I was getting what I deserved for ruining her life. I begged Daddy to let me stay with him or Nannie, but he just shook his head, saying I needed to be with my mother. I ran across the street and begged Nannie to take me. She looked at me with oceans of pity in her eyes.

"Little girl, as much as I would love to have you stay, you can't." Tears streamed like rivers down her wrinkled cheeks. "It wouldn't be right. You need to be with your family."

"I want you to be my family."

She glanced at the chaotic house across the street and got down on her knees.

"I wish I could be your family. You've been the best company I could ever ask for, and I'm going to miss you like you wouldn't believe. Remember everything that I told you, okay?"

I nodded solemnly.

Nannie lifted my chin, "I mean it, ya hear?"

"Will Nannie," I whispered with a quivering lip.

"Remember that God loves you. Remember that no matter what people do to you. You've got a light inside you that no one can touch as long as you don't let them." She hugged me tightly. "I love you, always."

"GET OVER HERE ASTRID!"

I held her tightly to me. I didn't want to leave her. "I love you too, Nannie."

"NOW ASTRID!"

"Go, little girl, before your mother has a stroke."

The trip from my old house to my Grandpa's house was long. At first, it was exciting. I saw places I had heard about but never seen. Eventually, all the houses and buildings turned into barns and crops, and I fell asleep. When Grace woke me for a bathroom break, I looked around, and there were still nothing but crops as far as the eye could see. I thought we would never get to Illinois.

On the way back to the car, Grandpa asked if I wanted to sit up front with him. He felt bad that he didn't know me very well and wanted to make up for it. Mom didn't look happy about sitting in the back seat, but didn't say anything. Feeling the tension, I didn't say much different at first. I was afraid to say something to make Mom madder.

He must have felt the tension too because he didn't say anything either. We just smiled at each other and watched the road stretching out before us. Not long after we got back on the road, I heard Grace's rhythmic breathing and Mom's light snoring. Grandpa must've seen this as a sign of safety too, because he started asking questions about me.

"So, Astrid, how old are you?" He glanced over with a warm smile.

"Four," I whispered, checking on Mom.

"Has your mother taught you anything about Jesus?"

My eyes widened, and I checked Mom again. "No, but my Nannie did."

"Who's Nannie?"

"The lady across the street. She used to tell me stories and help me remember certain sentences so that they could help me later."

"You went over there a lot."

I nodded, not daring to verbalize the truth. He grimaced, shaking his head. "Don't worry about her; she sleeps like the dead in the car."

The next several hours were spent listening to his stories. Most I hadn't heard, but he retold a few. His voice was rich, and its deep cadence soothed me. I didn't fall asleep, but I felt a calmness I usually found at Nannie's. It gave me a reason to hope this new place would mean a better life for me.

That hope died when I met my Grandma and aunt Sally. They cooed over Grace like she was a princess, then scowled at me like I was a toad. They were cut from the same cloth as my Mom, and they all seemed to hate me.

Grandma looked me over, with pursed lips. "Your mother has told us a lot about you. Are you going to cause trouble while you're here?"

"No, ma'am."

"Good." She crossed her arms. "I put up with BS. If you step out of line, I've got a switch with your name on it. Do you understand me?"

"Yes, ma'am."

"Good. Go get your stuff out of the car, and your mother will show you where you can put it."

With another 'Yes, ma'am' I went to the car. Mom was dividing the boxes into piles based on who's they were. So far, there were only a couple of boxes for me and half a dozen for Grace and Mom. I sat down in the grass and patiently waited for her to finish. When the car was cleaned out, I only had three boxes.

"Grab one of your boxes, and I'll show you your room."

"Okay."

I grabbed the one closest to me and followed Mom through the house. We passed two bedrooms and headed for the kitchen. On the other side of the kitchen was a laundry room. Mom pulled the chain, illuminating a rollaway bed in the corner with one chest of drawers that had seen better days.

"Things are going to be a little tight around here with all of us living here. So we had to make room for you in here."

"Why can't I sleep with Grace?"

Her lip curled. "Because she doesn't need to share a room with you. Besides, after what you did to me, you should be happy that you even have a bed."

My bottom lip quivered. "Okay."

"What do you say?"

"Thank you, mom."

"Go get the rest of your stuff, you ungrateful child."

I might have only been four, but even I could see a pattern forming. Things were getting worse for me. At least at the old house, I had my own room. I bit my lip determined not to cry. Tears would only make it worse. Taking a deep breath, I remembered one of the sayings Nannie taught me: "Rejoice in hope, patient in tribulation, continuing steadfastly in prayer."

With three harpies watching me, there wasn't anything they didn't notice, except when Grace did something. They didn't see anything she did wrong. When it wasn't something they could easily ignore, it ended up being something I did. So I would have to pick my switch.

After Mom got settled in and found a job, I saw less of her. She would take Grace out on days off and buy her new clothes or take her to the movies. I would stay home with my Grandma and aunt helping with the cleaning. On the good days, it wasn't so bad. Once I got my chores done and done well, they would let me play in the dollhouse in the backyard. I tried to savor those days because they were usually followed by days of yelling, slapping and swatting.

Grandpa didn't know about anything that was going on. He still worked, and by the time he got home, everyone had mellowed out. It wasn't until my aunt broke my arm that he started to realize something was wrong. I had just started school, and she made the comment that it was a good thing I had another arm, so

I could still do my schoolwork.
Between the disjointed story of
how my arm got broken and her
strange comment, I had never a
man get so red in my whole life.
It wasn't long after this episode
that I started throwing up on a
regular basis.

2

I could go into great detail about the next two years living with my Mom and her family, but it would only be a list of injuries. I thought the night my Grandpa got angry about my broken arm would change things for me, but it didn't. In fact, it was like throwing gas on a fire. Whatever Grandma or Mom told him worked to smooth everything over, and he popped his head right back into the sand. I was on my own.

By the time I was six, my mom had found a babysitter for my sister and I who wasn't a psychopath. She was an extremely nice older lady who colored and played games with us. Plus, in a strange twist of fate, she liked me better than my sister. Going to her house was like entering a

parallel universe. I couldn't
help feeling disappointed when my
Mom picked us up.

For the next two years, things
weren't good, but they never had
been for me. At least I had found
someone to shed light on my
gloomy days. Amy was a younger
version of Nannie. She was a
woman of faith and loved nature.
We would lie out in her backyard,
playing games, listening to her
read, or looking for shapes in
the clouds. It felt good to have
someone care about how I was
doing.

When I started school, I had
hoped that would be another place
I could take solace, but it
wasn't. The nuns at the Catholic
school were crabby spinsters who
seemed more interested in
punishing students for imagined
infractions than teaching. I
hated it there, and I dreaded it
so much, I vomited regularly.
After a month or so of this, my
Grandpa was able to persuade my
mother to take me to the doctor.
When he couldn't find an
explanation, my mother determined
I was looking for attention. My
constant ailment was just one
more thing for mother and the
harpies to complain about.
Eventually, life settled into a

new but familiar if miserable mediocrity with a sprinkle of kindness from Amy.

One day near the end of the school year, my father showed up at our house with a new family in tow. He introduced her to me and my sister as our "new mom." It was impossible, even for a six-year-old, to miss the triumphant look on my Dad's face, or the slightly green look of my mother's. I couldn't help feeling excited about the prospect of having a new mother. I longed for a home life like the other kids at school. I wanted hugs, family photos, and family game nights.

I made sure to mind my manners when I greeted Lynda and Molly. Lynda seemed nice and genuinely interested in learning all about me. That was a step up from my first mom. Molly was shy and didn't say much beyond "hi" at first. Over the course of the day she loosened up, and we ended up playing in the dollhouse. I couldn't stop myself from hoping they would take me away.

At first, I thought Dad was there to visit us. It had been two years since he had seen us. I thought maybe it had been a while because it was expensive to come to Illinois. It turned out I was

slow on the uptake. Watching Dad
flaunt his new wife in front of
Mom made me realize the visit was
nothing more than an opportunity
for Dad to shove his "happiness"
in her face. He wanted her to
feel replaced, and it worked. Mom
was so beside herself; she spent
most of their visit subdued.

After a few days, Dad and his
new family went back to Oklahoma.
Mom's newfound pensiveness lasted
for a couple of days after they
left. It also seemed to have
spread to my grandmother and
aunt. Those couple of days were
the most pleasant I had ever
spent in their house. They left
me alone. It made me wish my Dad
could visit more often.
Unfortunately, the bubble burst
and they were back to their usual
selves.

A couple of months later, Mom
came to my rollaway bed to let me
know she and Dad decided I would
go live with him. She was tired
of looking at me and dealing with
me, so it was his turn to suffer.
I didn't know how to feel about
that. I loved my Dad, but I
didn't know him that well either.
At the same time, I figured it
had to be better than here.

Within two weeks, my bags were
packed, and Dad picked me up. On

the way to Oklahoma, we talked a lot and got to know each other. The more we talked, the more hopeful I got about my future. Despite being happy about leaving, a part of me missed my sister. She could be a pain, but it was weird not having her with me. I couldn't help but wonder what Mom was going to do when stuff got broke, or a chore didn't get done, and I wasn't there to blame and beat for it.

Lynda and Molly were waiting for me when we pulled into the driveway of an average white house on the edge of town. They welcomed me with tight hugs and cheerful greetings, and it was a nice feeling I wasn't used to. With her arm wrapped around me, Lynda showed me to my new room. I unpacked my duffle bag, meticulously putting my wrinkled clothes into the drawer and closet. I was determined to earn their love, and I wanted to start things off on the right foot.

That first night was sadly amazing. We sat at the table and ate dinner like a family. We cleared off the table, and they taught me how to play Go-Fish. I got to sleep in a regular bed in my own room. The weight of the world had come off my shoulders;

I had a loving home. For the first time in my whole life, my future seemed bright.

Then the other shoe dropped. Even now, I can't say for sure what I did or didn't do that started the chain of events that would govern my life for the next ten years. I do remember it was about a month after I came to Oklahoma. It was a typical warm summer day with not a cloud in the sky. I had been playing all day, and I didn't come in until I heard my Dad come home.

It was later than when he usually came home, but I didn't think anything of it. Sometimes he worked late. He seemed a little unsteady on his feet, leaning precariously against the refrigerator door while he grabbed a beer. I could tell that Lynda wasn't as happy to see him as usual. He barely spared me a glance before slamming the refrigerator door and heading to the living room.

The house was full of tension. Dinner that night was quiet. My Dad gave no more than one-word answers to anything that any of us said. He ate faster than usual and as soon as he was done, grabbed another beer and headed back to the living room. That night was the first time I had ever seen my father's chair surrounded by beer cans. It was also the first time I never heard my Dad and Lynda fight.

Lynda yelled, my Dad yelled. I'm not sure how long they argued. Lynda must have said something my father particularly didn't appreciate because I heard something hit the floor, and Lynda didn't reply. I heard his footsteps coming down the hall. Instead of passing my room, he stopped at my door. I could see the shadow of his feet dancing under the door. The scene reminded me of my Mom's friend John just before he would come into my room. A cold shiver went down my spine. After a couple of minutes, his footsteps continued down the hall.

From that time on, it was nothing to see Dad surrounded by beer cans after dinner. The evenings of playing games were gone. In fact, playing with us at all was gone. It seemed as the summer wore on, the looks my father gave us, especially me, grew more contemptuous. I racked my brain trying to figure out what I had done to make him so mad. My mother's voice would pop in my head reminding me that I'm just unlovable.

My heart broke at the idea my father hated me as much as my mother. Despite not knowing what I had done to make someone mad, I tried to do things better than I had before. I tried to do my chores better. I paid closer attention to my manners. I even paid attention to when his beer was gone so I could bring him a fresh one at just the right time. Nothing I tried made a difference. He always seemed to be looking at me with disgusted disappointment.

The bloom fell off my relationship with my "new mom" too. It seemed like out of nowhere my relationship with Lyn'da turned into the same relationship I had with my mom. Nothing was ever good enough. Anything Molly did was my fault because her daughter would know better, and I was either slapped or swatted with the switch. I was back to square one.

My life took on the cadence of misery it had in Illinois, except I liked my sister better than Molly. While I always got the blame for Grace's behavior, she didn't try to get me in trouble. The longer we lived together, the more Molly would do, and the worse my punishments from my "new mom" would get. I was relieved when school started again, but I was disappointed that it was another Catholic school. As I expected, these nuns were the same as the nuns in Illinois: angry, self-righteous spinsters. While I hated school, I did make friends. The girls in Oklahoma were much friendlier than in Illinois.

Everything came to a head after I lived in Oklahoma for about six months. Daddy had been drinking, which was normal. I always felt like he was watching me like he was reconnoitering an enemy. I tried to ignore it and act like everything was normal. I still maintained my vigil of anticipating when he would make his next appearance, trying desperately to get on his good side again. He took the cans with suspicion and dismissed me. Taking back my seat on the floor, I went back to my book.

"Astrid, did you tell your Dad what happened in school?" Lynda's condescending voice echoed behind me.

I slowly looked up from the book where I was doing more hiding than reading. My father's eyes narrowed. I blushed, sitting up and setting the book aside.

"What happened, Astrid?" Dad's voice was low and tight.

I glanced at him before looking at the shag carpet. "I got sick, Daddy, and threw up today."

"Did they send you home?" He slammed his empty beer can down on the end table.

"N…N..No, Lyn-." My eyes stared to Lynda's hateful ones. "No, I convinced them that I would be okay. I told them that I get sick like that sometimes. It must've been something I ate."

"I think," she pinned me with another scathing glare, "this is your way of getting attention. Like you don't get enough already."

"No, I'm not!" The statement came out before I could stop myself and more forcefully than I wanted.

My father nearly jumped from his chair. "Don't you take that tone with your mother! She has to put up with a lot from you! The least you could do is show some respect! Go to your room!" My Dad pointed to the hallway.

Tears welled in my eyes." I'm sorry." I whispered and headed to my room.

I went to my room with my head hung, wondering who would come to hit me. I waited for a long time on my bed like a death row inmate waiting for his first injection, but nobody came. Dad and Lynda were fighting. When eight o'clock rolled around, I started to get ready for bed. By 8:30, I had said my prayers and thanked Jesus for making them fight so they would forget me.

The dipping of the bed woke me up. The scent of stale beer filled my nose. I sleepily tried to turn over, but something stopped me. I bolted up to see the slightly moonlit face of my blurry-eyed father.

"You are so much like your mother," he groused, and gently touched my cheek.

The hair on the back of my neck stood on end. Even being young, I understood that wasn't necessarily a compliment. In a split second my cheek stung, and my head swam.

His body shifted and his breath washed over me. My warm blanket was yanked off me, leaving me vulnerable to the chill in the

air. That night, the father of my
childhood died, and the monster
took over.

3

It was probably due to my
mother's "conditioning," but
being hit by my father or Lynda
didn't bother me as it probably
should have. What bothered me was
the way my father coldly
brutalized me. There is a
different type of shame that
comes with being sexually abused
by someone you trust, especially
a parent. It is a combination of
being ashamed you share part of
your DNA with the person and
allowing him to make you feel so
powerless that you have to endure
in silence.

After the first night, my
father abused me regularly.
Sometimes it was physical
punches, and kicks, and sometimes
it was sexual. He loved to remind
me after each sexual assault that

if I ever told anyone about it, he would kill me. The glint in his eye when he said it told me it wasn't an idle threat. It also told me it wouldn't be quick. He'd want me to suffer for a while before I died, so I could truly appreciate what I had done wrong.

From the time I was seven till twelve, I endured a steady diet of abuse. The times I didn't bear bruises or discomfort from either my father or Lynda were few and far between. Those times usually coincided with my father's occasional business trips. During those times, Lynda seemed more gentle. She didn't speak any better to me, but she left me alone more.

After the first year, Molly usually gave me a wide berth. Most of the time, I only saw her in the morning and at dinner time. This arrangement suited me just fine because the less time we spent in the same room, the less chance there was I would be blamed for her crimes.

I don't know if my father got bored with what he was doing to me, or he had seen something somewhere, but around the time I was eleven or twelve, he added to his depravity. Now my abuse was the worst kept secret. The teachers, *nuns,* knew something was wrong. My friends knew, and there was no doubt the doctors knew, but no one said a word. They looked at me with pity, patched me up and sent me down the road. That gave my father a sense of invincibility.

It started with Lynda's parents' house. Lynda and my father regularly went there to play cards. Molly went to her grandparents' room to watch TV. I wasn't far behind when my father jerked me back by the shoulder. My heart jumped into my throat, and I spun around. A sinister grin played on his lips, making me want to vomit. In his hand was a brown leather dog collar.

"Put this on,"

I stared at the collar and looked at him. I was sure I was misunderstanding. The Joker-like grin faded into the familiar one of rage – barely controlled rage.

"You heard me, Astrid. Put the collar on and come sit by me. NOW!"

"I – I don't under-," suddenly I was on the floor with a throbbing cheek and the taste of copper in my mouth.

33

"You don't need to understand. I'm your Dad. I'm the boss, and you're going to be my dog." He dropped the collar on me. "Now, do it."

For the first time in my whole life, I wished for a simple beating. Somehow getting kicked and punched hurt less than being humiliated. Physical injuries heal over time, but humiliation like this, it lives in your soul. I was out of my depth, and I prayed to God that he would protect me from whatever was coming next.

My father took his seat at the dining room table and started shuffling cards like it was normal to have your kid collared. With tears running down my cheek, obstructing my vision, I put the collar around my neck. Lynda, Cheryl, and Al ignored me and focused on small talk, but I could feel my father watching me.

"Make sure it's tight Astrid."

"Yes, sir." I murmured numbly.

"Good."

"Astrid! Come here, girl. Come sit next to me." He motioned at me like someone would do for a dog to come.

With my head down, I took a step toward him. "Get on your hands and knees. Dogs don't walk on just two legs."

I glanced up waiting for someone to say something. Lynda, Cheryl, and Al were intently arranging their cards. Seconds felt like months. The longer my father waited for my compliance, the darker his face got. With another mumbled 'Yes, sir' I got down on my hands and knees.

I made my way across the blue high-pile carpet leaving tears behind. It took everything I had to keep my sobs back and my body still. When I reached his knee, he jerked my head up by my hair.

"Kneel next to me with your head down. Don't talk unless you are spoken to by me, and if I need anything from the kitchen, you'll get it for me on your hands and knees. Got it?"

"Yes, sir."

He let go of my hair and backhanded me in the blink of an eye. "Now you have a reason to cry."

I thought that night was a one-off, but it wasn't. From that night on, it was a new part of the torment. I would be collared next to him during dinners, while

he watched TV, when they had
company, and even at the homes of
their friends. I was angry, not
just at him for doing it but for
no one sticking up for me. I
couldn't believe people would
allow someone to treat a child
like that. It was a hard lesson I
had to learn: nobody from the
outside will help you. People
aren't going to put themselves
out there for you.

After another year, I tried to
talk to Lynda's mother about what
was going on. I was hoping if I
told her everything that was
going on, she would find it in
her heart to help me. Instead,
she worried about what would
happen to her daughter if it got
out her husband was a depraved
man. She even went as far as to
say that her daughter and my
father hitting me was deserved. I
was floored. Considering how many
times they had seen my father or
Lynda hit me or kick me for no
real reason, I couldn't believe
she said that with a straight
face.

As it turned out, I should've
known better than to say anything
to her. She didn't even keep my
confidence a full day before she
told her daughter what I said. Of
course, Lynda told my father when

he came home from work. He wasted
no time coming to my room and
giving me the most savage beating
of my life, up to that point. I
was so battered and bruised that
I couldn't go to school for two
weeks.

I had a lot of time to think
while I was recovering. I
couldn't figure out why I was
left in the lurch. How can some
watch a child be *punched* and
kicked for no reason other than
forgetting to turn on the dryer
or a wet towel left on the floor?
How can you watch that and say
nothing? Then, it occurred to me.
Cheryl didn't want to get
involved because she didn't want
people to know her daughter had
poor taste in men. Lynda didn't
say anything about the sexual
abuse because she figured as long
as he was occupied with me, he
would leave her daughter alone.
The teachers, doctors, the
cashier at the grocery store,
didn't say anything because they
didn't want to get into other
peoples' business. So my job was
basically to protect everyone
else's sensibilities no matter
what it cost me.

Whether it was a conscious
decision or not, I'm still not
sure, I stopped going right home

after school. Instead, I would go to the library at the local college. I loved to read. It was a great escape from reality. I also loved the smell of books. It's the smell of knowledge and opportunity. The library was a quiet place where I could peacefully work on my homework and think. I went there because I felt safe. You know your life is messed up when a college campus is safer for you than home.

I think the reason I started to rebel was I had nothing to lose. What were they going to do? Hit me? That was already a near-daily part of my life. When they didn't hurt me, I was sick – vomiting till I was dry heaving. What else could they do to me? I suppose they could've killed me but where is the fun in that? Plus, a corpse can't protect children and middle-aged women's reputations. For once, I was going to do something for me.

When I finally meandered home that first night around 7:30 or so, I got beat up by Lynda. Dad was out of town for work. Maybe that's why I decided to do it; I'm not sure. The look on Lynda's face when I told her I was at the library was priceless. She looked like I had told her I was on the corner downtown hookin.' I took the beating though, and it was worth the peace and solitude.

I suppose I could have made it easier on myself by asking for permission instead of just taking off, but I knew they would never give it. By thirteen, I was used to the abuse. So every time I went to the library after school or during the summer, I would come home to a whipping from Lynda. As strange as it sounds, I didn't even realize they were getting worse until she broke a couple of my fingers on my left hand and dislocated my right shoulder. There was something about that beating that "concerned" my father. Apparently, even monsters have their limits.

I was getting settled into bed. The hospital had given me some amazing pain medication, so I was feeling good and relaxed. Without knocking, my father walked into my room. My stomach dropped, and my heart sped up. He only came into my room for one thing. Hanging my head, I dropped onto my bed. It was an instant response to seeing him there. Be compliant, go to your "happy" place until he's done. The realization made me wonder if I was a dog.

With the gentlest touch he had given me in years, my father lifted my head. The look on his face was … contrite? Maybe sad? When I looked into his eyes, they were as cold and hard as a great white shark's. I shivered while a tear escaped the corner of my blackened eye.

"She really did a number on ya kiddo." His lip almost curled into a smile.

I nodded, unsure of how to reply.

He took a seat next to me and tucked some hair behind my ear. "You need to stop making her so angry. Most dogs only have to be beaten a few times to learn. Why are you stupider than an animal?"

I shrugged. Talks like this with my father could end with a punch or a slap for speaking out of turn. I couldn't figure out where he was going with the conversation. Did he want honesty? Did he want me to just say "I'm sorry and I'll never do it again?" I was sore, tired, and scared.

"Answer me, Astrid."

"I just want to go to the library," I whispered.

"Yeah, okay, the library."

"No Dad, that's really where I go. Sometimes I go by myself, and sometimes I go with Julie."

"Okay, well, this is the deal. I can't keep Lynda away from you. If you can't fly right and stop making her angry, then you deserve what you get. At the rate you're going, you're going to end up with an extended stay at the hospital."

I nodded.

"The next time she hits you. Hit her back. Beat her down. Don't stop till she quits moving. If you don't start defending yourself, I'll take you out back and put one between your eyes. Do you understand me?"

I couldn't believe what I was hearing. Instead of taking it because I deserve it, my father was telling me I better fight back – or else. I was sure it was some trick, but I didn't understand why. What I did understand perfectly was my father's promise to kill me if I didn't fight back.

I nodded again, and he left the room. I sighed and finished

getting ready for bed. That night was long and sleepless. Between my injuries and what my father had said to me, my mind was spinning with all kinds of thoughts and feelings.

The next few days were spent mostly in solitude. I stayed in my room for the most part, reading and listening to the radio. I would come out for food, drink, and the bathroom. When Lynda got off work, she would leave me alone, but she seemed conflicted while doing it. My father watched us both intently. I didn't realize it at the time, but this was the calm before the storm.

A week or so later, Lynda came home in a particularly bad mood. Pots, pans, and cupboard doors were slamming around in the kitchen. I dreaded getting up for dinner that night. Dinner time could be precarious in the best of times, but when either Lynda or my father was already agitated, it could be explosive. Since I was sore enough already, I decided to act like I was asleep.

Just as my eyes closed, my door slammed open. Without ceremony, Lynda grabbed me by the hair and drug me to the kitchen.

"I've had a long day, and since you have been lazing about all day, you can make dinner."

I scanned the kitchen for a moment trying to figure out what I could make. I turned to ask Lynda what she wanted when something hit me in the side of the head. Dazed, I stumbled back into the counter. I barely got my bearings before she hit me in the stomach. My father's words echoed in my head.

Prickling fear ran through me like icy rivers. I was afraid of what would happen if I fought back and I was afraid of what would surely happen if I didn't. Mustering all the strength I had, I ran down the hall to my room. The locked door didn't stop Lynda. With superhuman-like strength, she broke open my door. Her eyes were like brimstone. I knew one way or the other I would die that night if I didn't do something.

Channeling everything inside me, all my anger, sadness, loneliness, and pain, I curled my small fist and hit her with all of it. I connected perfectly with her jaw. Between the shock and the force of my hit, she dropped. I jumped on her, pummeling her face.

I'm not sure how many shots I got in before strong hands jerked me up. "Get off her, Astrid."

My face felt like white-hot fire. I panted and shook with the force of emotions coursing through me. I became a spectator in my own body. I couldn't stop hitting her; everything poured out of me. I heard my father's voice in the distance, demanding I stop, but I carried on until I was wrenched from her.

Despite pulling me off his wife, he didn't seem angry. In fact, he almost seemed … proud. There was an approving glint in his eye that I had never seen before. A small smile tugged at the corner of his mouth, and he slapped me on the back.

Lynda was another story. It took her a few minutes to pull herself off the floor, but when she did – she let Dad, as well as the neighbors, know how she felt. Dabbing daintily at her nose with a towel, Lynda glared at me.

"Either she leaves, or I do!" A hardened gaze fell on Dad. "I have put up with so much. I refuse to be her punching bag. You better get her out of here. Now!"

My body tingled with fear. I had no idea where Dad would take me. Surprisingly, he had nothing to say about her ultimatum. He grabbed my hand and took me toward the door. Not breaking his stride, he grabbed the keys on the kitchen counter, and we were out the side door.

The rumble of his truck's engine was the only sound for quite a while. I had no idea where we were going, and I did not have the strength or courage to ask. Honestly, I was still reveling in the relief that he was unarmed.

After about 15 minutes of uncomfortable silence, he said, "This really is for the best. I mean …. Believe it or not, I've tried to keep her off you, but….," He trailed off into a shrug.

I nodded, absently staring out the window. I wasn't sure how wherever he was taking me would be better. His family was just as crazy as him, so I couldn't imagine a better life there. Dread knotted in my stomach at the thought of him taking me back to my mother. I was so consumed with fear and uncertainty at the thought, I didn't realize we had stopped until he got out.

We were at the grocery store. Without a word, he headed in. Part of me wanted to make a run for it. What did I have to lose. There were lots of places to hide on campus. I could get by for a few days to figure out what to do next. Instead, I sat there with bated breath, wondering what my father was up to now.

He came out with a carton of Marlboro Reds and a green lighter. I arched a curious eyebrow at the strange purchases. My father didn't smoke those. With a tight smile, he motioned for me to get out. Cautiously I slid out of the truck.

"These are for you."

My eyes shifted from the carton of cigarettes to my father, trying to figure out was going on. I didn't smoke.

He shook the carton at me. "Take 'em."

I timidly took the carton, holding it to my chest, and stuffed the lighter in my pocket. "Wh-."

"This is the best thing for you. It really is." He climbed into the truck. "If anyone can make it, it would be you."

My brain disconnected. I was so overwhelmed; I shut down. Without a goodbye, my father left me in the store parking lot. He released me. A million different emotions washed over me, the strongest of them were relief and fear. I knew this was too good to be true.

The parking lot was practically deserted, but I was afraid of drawing someone attention. So I headed to the far corner of the parking lot. I stared at the carton as I sat on the curb. I never tried smoking; it always seemed like a smelly and dirty habit. However, they were the only things I had besides the clothing on my back, so I opened it and pulled out my first pack. It took me a couple of cigarettes to get the hang of it, but I eventually figured out how to inhale without choking.

Looking back on it, I'm not sure why he gave me the cigarettes. Ten or twenty bucks would've been more useful. Then again, maybe that's why. Maybe he thought giving me cash would make my survival too easy. Or maybe he thought it would help relieve the stress of being abandoned by him. My father, it was hard telling.

I wasn't even 13, so there was no way to stay at a motel. I had a few friends, but their parents would ask too many questions and would probably take me home. By the time I finished my third cigarette, I had resolved to walk to the college and hide out in the bathroom at one of the dorms till morning. I had no idea what to do from there, but at least I had somewhere to be for the night.

I had only made it a half a dozen steps when my Dad's truck pulled up next to me. My body went rigid. He had been gone for less than a half-hour, and I knew that wasn't a good sign. Either this was some joke or a test. Regardless, I knew it would end badly for me. The question was "what was he going to do to me?"

"Get in, Astrid."

Not trusting my voice, I nodded and came around the front and got in. My father had a huge grin on his face as we pulled out of the parking lot.

"I found somewhere else to take you."

A chill went down my spine. "Where?" I whispered.

"You'll see."

It was a short drive to the local youth shelter downtown. The shelter was a medium-sized brick building with a chipped white sign in front. A tall white light illuminated the sidewalk in front of a single glass door. It looked like it might've been a doctor's office in its previous life.

My mouth hung open. Again, I was overwhelmed. I had heard stories in school about the kids here. They were dirty, and they were rough. They swore. They drank. They fought. While I didn't want to come home, I didn't want to live in a shelter with these strange, possibly violent kids.

"Come on."

I couldn't move. I want.... Fear of the unknown paralyzed me. It was hard to imagine living there could be any more precarious than living with Dad and Lynda, but sometimes it's the devil you know. I knew how to survive in that madhouse, but I wasn't sure I could survive here.

"Get out of the car, Astrid!"

I jumped at the tone in his voice and immediately got out. Clutching my cigarettes to my chest, I followed my father into the shelter. I wanted to make him take me home, but nothing came out of my mouth. Even if I had begged, it wouldn't have mattered. Once my Dad had something in his head, he was determined to do it.

The air smelled sterile, almost like a hospital, but with an undertone of body odor. With a handful of chairs and a small table covered in magazines, the reception area reminded me of the doctor's office. I timidly took a seat on one of the worn chairs. An unfriendly looking woman glared at us from the reception desk.

"How can I help you?"

"Hi, my name is Richard Clark." That sounded almost chipper. "I'm bringing my daughter, Astrid Clark, in tonight because she had an altercation with her stepmother."

The receptionist eyed me cautiously, "Did you call the police?"

"No," he looked over his shoulder at me pensively, "I didn't want her to get charged with anything, but she can't stay with us anymore."

The woman scrutinized me as my father spun his tale. His story painted me as a juvenile delinquent that they couldn't deal with anymore. It was total BS, but my father was so convincing, I almost believed I was a delinquent.

The receptionist crossed her arms, "Are we going to have any trouble from you, young lady?"

"No, ma'am," I whispered.

Her expression softened slightly. She grabbed a clipboard and gave it to my father. Within 20 minutes, he had completed the intake paperwork and was waving goodbye as I was being escorted through the solid oak door behind the receptionist's desk.

4

Staying at the shelter was
great. The kids were all friendly
enough. They were all rough
around the edges, but considering
where we were, it was
understandable. We slept in bunk
beds, four girls to a room. Meg
was one of my roommates. We hit
it off. We both liked to read and
enjoyed talking about the books
we read. She had explained her
family problems and what led her
to the shelter. I had to bite my
tongue to keep from telling her
she was just a spoiled brat. She
asked about me, but I always
hedged around the facts or
changed the subject.

Meg had lived at the shelter
for a couple of weeks, and helped
me learn the ropes. We all had
chores to do every day. When the

work was done, we could hang out in the common room and watch TV or go back to our room. If Meg was busy, I would sit outside and read. It was against the rules, but since Miss Ellen knew I had no intention of leaving, she let me.

For the first time in a long time, I felt safe. When I went to sleep each night, I didn't do so rigid with fear. I didn't worry that I would be attacked in the middle of the night. I enjoyed a deep, rejuvenating sleep while I was at the shelter. I relished that time, and I hoped it was the start of a new life for me. Somewhere in the back of my mind, I knew it wouldn't last.

It had been nearly three weeks since my father left me at the shelter. I had established a routine there. I would eat breakfast, do my chores, and have the rest of the day to do whatever. On that day the sun was bright, but the breeze was cool. I was sunning myself while I smoked a cigarette. A copy of Dante's <u>The Divine Comedy</u> lying next to me. It was a perfect day.

A familiar rumble caught my attention. My heart immediately thumped against my chest. I kept my eyes closed. I didn't want to

see what I already knew was
there. My father. He was back.
Taking a deep breath, I opened my
eyes.

I saw his truck pull into a
spot. My stomach roiled, and
tears welled. I knew it was too
good to be true. I knew he would
be back at some point. I bit my
lip to keep it from quivering and
dashed the tears away. I didn't
want to give him the satisfaction
of seeing my fear.

"Hey kiddo," he smiled,
"Enjoying those smokes?"

I nodded and tossed my
cigarette as I followed him
inside. I prayed he wasn't there
to take me away. The idea of
going back to that house was
killing my stomach. Now that I
had tasted peace, I couldn't
stand the thought of going back
to that violent, chaotic house. I
sat in the same worn chair I had
sat in three weeks before while
I, again, waited to see what he
had in store for me.

"Hi, my name is Richard Clarke.
How are you today?"

"Good, thank you, Mr. Clarke,"
Miss Ellen replied congenially,
"What can I do for you today?"

"I have been informed by my
wife that my daughter has taken

some of her clothing. She would like me to get them back." I could hear his charming smile.

"Oh?" Miss Ellen's eyes shifted to me questioningly. I shrugged because I didn't know what he was talking about either.

"Yeah," he chuckled, "It's just one more example of the problems we've been having with Astrid. Can I get them or can someone bring me her things?"

My hands began shaking. This was a way for him to show me that he was always in control. He always had power over me, no matter where I was. He might allow me freedom from time to time, but I would never be free of him.

"Ummm, Mr. Clarke, that isn't possible since she only came in here with the clothes on her back. Everything she has now is because the shelter has provided it."

"I'm telling you," his voice deepened as his temper flared, "she has some of my wife's clothes, and she wants them back. Now!" He slammed his hand down on the desk.

Miss Ellen's face twisted with disdain. "*Again*, Mr. Clarke, Astrid doesn't have anything that

the shelter, didn't provide
except for the cigarettes. *You,
sir,* left her with nothing. I
suggest you and your wife check
Astrid's room at home because she
has nothing here."

My father leaned in menacingly,
"CHECK.HER.ROOM." His voice was
deathly low.

The look on his face must have
been fierce because she paled and
there was an audible gulp. The
room filled with a frighteningly
familiar tension. She shuffled
paper and such around the desk,
avoiding my father's piercing
stare.

She finally peeked at him,
"Fine." Her voice was soft and
tremulous. "Follow me." She
glanced at me, fear evident in
her eyes, "Come on, Astrid."

Nodding, I followed a couple of
paces behind them to my room. I
wasn't worried. I saw this for
what it was, a game. He was there
to show me that even when I'm
somewhere else, I'm always under
his thumb.

Once we were in my room, he
wasted no time tearing through my
dresser. My clean clothes were
tossed on the floor. Paying no
mind to them, he trampled them
while checking each drawer. A

sinister chuckle erupted as he dumped the last drawer. He turned with a triumphant smile and a couple of my stepmother's T-shirts in his hand.

"Look what I found."

Miss Ellen put her arm around my shoulders and sighed, "I'm telling you those aren't your wife's. All of our clothes are donations. Those shirts are ones we gave her. I assure you."

He ignored her, focusing on me. "It's time for you to go. I think you need to go somewhere where they can handle you."

Without another word to Miss Ellen, he jerked me out of the room. I stupidly tried to plant my feet and pull myself away, but his grip tightened. His nails dug into my forearm as he dragged me through the shelter.

"Where are we going?"

He flung me toward the truck door, "I'm taking you somewhere else, and that's all you need to know. Get in!"

My stomach roiled. Deep down, I knew wherever I was going wasn't a place I wanted to be. He must have smelled my contentment at the shelter. My stomach felt worse as we left town. I knew better than to question him further when he had such an evil look on his face.

Several long, tense hours and three states later we were in Kentucky; more specifically, a prison-like like girls' home. It was a large brick building built sometime in the last century. In reality, it looked no different than some schools I had seen, but it had an ominous aura. Tears blurred my vision.

He dragged me out of the truck and up the stairs. Despite being scared, I wasn't giving him any trouble. His pushiness was another move in the game. It was designed to help him spin his tale about me.

"Please don't make me come here," I sniffed, "I'll do anything that you want me to do if you just take me home."

"That's not gonna happen," he grinned, "Your stepmother is still pretty upset with you. I think it's better for everyone if you go somewhere else. Besides, you still need to learn who's boss."

We were met by Mr. Brubaker, the headmaster of the school. While talking to Mr. Brubaker, my father spun a taller tale. He told him about beating up my stepmother, which was true. He also told Mr. Brubaker that I was a thief, a runaway and that I had stabbed one of my aunts in a fit of rage. When my father said that, I think I looked just as surprised as Mr. Brubaker.

My father played the concerned, frazzled parent with ease. His charming manner and convincing speech made it easy for people to believe everything he said. The act was so good, I almost believed him. He should have been an actor; he would've won lots of Oscars.

Within an hour, the paperwork was done, and it was time for us to say goodbye. I could've just walked away. I didn't want to be there, and I didn't deserve it. Being here was just another punishment for another imagined crime.

My father touched my shoulder. He looked at me in a way I can't describe. It was almost … apologetic.

"If you want to survive here, you better be ready to fight. You better win. If I find out anything different, I'll beat you till you wish you were dead."

I wanted to ask how that would be any different than any other time, but I knew that wasn't wise. With a tear escaping, I simply nodded. I scanned the stark, drab hallway. There were a couple of girls dusting and a couple cleaning the floor. They looked like they had seen a lot, just like me. Strangely, I wasn't worried. Considering my home life, how much worse could it be? I felt as safe here as I ever did at "home."

With his signature smug smile, my father said, "See you later kid."

I had hoped it was an empty promise. I didn't care if he ever came back. After all the beatings and the rapes, I had no desire to see him or "home" again. I knew, though, he would be back. He couldn't leave me alone. I was like his favorite toy to abuse.

The school was only a small step above a prison. The uniforms we wore were made of a thick material that made me break out. They managed to find an older uniform that didn't bother me, but it took days for me to recover. It was icing on my turd cake.

My days were regimented: up at six a.m., breakfast at seven, lunch at noon, and so on. We were only allowed outside during gym. We were assigned chore groups and our chores rotated each week. It was a depressing existence.

The one bright spot was meeting Kelly. She had a similar background to my own, except she did steal and was a frequent runaway. Even though our experiences were similar, it had shaped us differently. She was angry and felt like she was entitled to what she wanted because of all the hell she had been through. Despite our differences, we bonded over our love of reading.

While Kelly's company helped, I couldn't stand being there. I wasn't like the other girls. They were jaded and even violent. They were everything my father said I was, but I wasn't. I knew if I stayed there, I would end up just like them. I had to get out.

My escape was more of a whim than a plan. I had only been there a couple of weeks, but it was long enough to memorize routines. We were outside for gym. The teacher, Mrs. Smyth, would often have one of the older, trusted students watch us while she went to the bathroom. Fortunately, Marcy wasn't a vigilant babysitter. So while she was talking to one of her friends, I made a beeline for the trees. Beyond them was a section of stone wall with a vine-covered gate in a state of disrepair. I took that as God's blessing to get out of there. It didn't take much for me to squeeze between the wall and the crumbling bars. I ran down the street as fast as I could.

Since there was no planning for my escape, it didn't take long for school security to find me. I was on the side of a private road that led to the back entrance of the school. Unfortunately, they called my father to let him know what happened. He showed up the next day.

They had called me to the office. I figured they wanted to yell at me some more and pile on more punishments. I absently scratched at my arm as I reached the bottom of the stairs. I could hear him raging at the headmaster like I was already in the room. My stomach flipped, and I stumbled.

Blood roared in my ears while a million thoughts went through my head. My first coherent thought was to find somewhere to hide, but that would only get me in more trouble. There was no way to avoid this confrontation. The bright side was he couldn't beat me or anything like he would at home.

I kept my head down when I entered the room. He was still yelling at Mr. Brubaker; calling him and his staff every name in the book. It took my father a minute or two before he realized I was there. When he did, his diatribe stopped. The floor shook under his feet as he made his way toward me. Grabbing my arm, he forced me to look at him. The look he gave me was both familiar and dangerous. While my father's flinty eyes gripped me, Mr. Brubaker seemed to have melted away.

He shoved me, then backhanded me, "Did you *really* think you could get away with it, you little idiot?"

I stumbled but managed to stay on my feet. I kept silent, cradling my throbbing cheek. Tears welled, making it hard to see what he was doing.

"Answer me!" I could feel his stale breath on my other cheek before the back of my head exploded.

I fell to my knees, grabbing my head. My body shook with the force of my sobs. I could barely think between the confusion and the pain. Where was everyone? Surely they could hear what was going on. Were they really going to let him beat me? Suddenly, my head was wrenched from the floor, and I was staring at my father's cold eyes again.

"Answer. Me." He whispered menacingly, yanking my hair.

"I…I d-don't know," I wailed.

He shoved me, and I fell on my side. Towering over me, he watched me convulsively sob. I waited for more blows. He usually beat me till I quit moving, but he didn't this time. Instead, he knelt down, jerking my arm closer to his face.

"What's all over you?"

I shook my head. I had no idea what was on my arms. Whatever it was, it itched like crazy.

He studied it for a minute, before chuckling. "Looks like you've got poison ivy." He pushed me away, "Idiot."

I scratched my arm while I continued to snivel. When the

tears ran dry, I saw the rash that bloomed. It was an angry red that went from hands up to my elbow.

"I hope you learned your lesson." He towered over me again. "If you haven't and this happens again, I'll kill you." He grabbed me by the hair again, "Do you understand me? I. Will. Put. A. Bullet. Between. Your. Eyes."

I nodded vehemently, sobbing again.

He left me shaking in that office without a backward glance. I couldn't decide if I was happy or sad that I wasn't going with him. I didn't like the school, but I didn't like "home" either. At least if I went back to Oklahoma, I had a chance of getting away. I knew where I could hide there. I felt lost.

Mr. Brubaker had the secretary take me to the nurse. She confirmed that I had poison ivy. Nothing was said about my bruised face. The nurse simply gave me ice with pity in her eyes. They were kind enough to let me rest that day.

I spent the next week or so covered in calamine lotion. My normally free time was consumed with extra chores. I used that

time to think about where I went
wrong. Of course, my first
mistake was not making a plan,
but I also realized that getting
lost in the city wasn't going to
work. They knew where to look for
runaways. If I was going to get
away, I would need to be away
from people.

A couple of weeks after my ill-
fated escape, Kelly and I were
reading in the library. Kelly had
just finished a book I suggested,
Island of the Blue Dolphins. Not
only did she love it, but it gave
her an idea. We could live in the
woods. Looking back on it, that
idea was more ridiculous than my
idea to get lost in the city.
Back then, it sounded like a good
idea.

We decided to wait till lights
out on Sunday. We figured out
that was the least staffed day.
Once everything was quiet, and
the staff's guard was down, we
would sneak out and head for the
woods.

The door softly clicked open.
"Are you ready?"

"Yeah, let's go."

Flinging our backpacks over our
shoulders, we quickly headed to
the services stairs in our
stockinged feet. We took them

slowly to keep our footsteps from echoing. Thank God we were only on the second floor. We slipped out of the building, keeping our eyes peeled for people outside or in the windows.

The air was cool and refreshing, typical for October. I zipped my hoodie and sprinted to the tree line.

We didn't stop running until we were well into the woods. Kelly found a small clearing with a large tree stump on the eastern side. I pulled out a couple of apples that I had saved earlier in the week, handing one to Kelly.

Kelly stared at the apple absently. "What are we going to do now?"

I shrugged, "stay here in the woods till we're 18 then… I don't know."

"That's like five years away for you."

I nodded, "I know, but I don't have anywhere else to go."

"What about your mom?"

I snorted at the thought and took a bite of my apple. "My mom is crazy like my father. As far as I'm concerned, I'm an orphan."

Kelly picked at her apple peel, "I don't have anyone either. I'm here because my mom didn't believe me when I told her about her boyfriend. I started running away and hanging out with the wrong crowd because I didn't want to go home."

"No one ever believed me either." I gazed up at hazy sky. "My Mom didn't believe me about her boyfriend, and no one believed me about my Dad," I sighed. "Or if they did, they didn't do anything about it. Same difference."

Suddenly, the bushes across the way began to shake wildly. Kelly and I dropped our food and bolted. I'm not sure how long we ran but my legs ached, and my lungs felt like they would explode. Once my breathing return to normal, I noticed the sounds of traffic not far away. I tapped Kelly on the shoulder and motioned for her to follow me.

At about a quarter mile the trees broke to reveal a neighborhood. It was an average neighborhood. The homes weren't overly nice, but they were well-maintained. We stayed within the trees that followed the road.

"I think I recognize the street," Kelly bubbled behind me.

"Do you know how far away we are from the school?"

"I don't know … um …. Maybe a couple of miles."

I slumped. We weren't nearly as far as I hoped. Kelly tugged at my arm. I turned to see her beaming at one of the smaller houses on the block. It was white with brown trim and a large picture window in front.

"That's my friend's house," she said, pointing "I recognize the bumper sticker on her dad's truck!"

Following her finger, I saw a bumper sticker that read "Shit Happens."

"Let's go!" Kelly pulled me across the street toward the house.

We went around to the back door. She knocked, and I fidgeted with nervous energy. I didn't think this was a good idea. We needed to keep moving and find cover. It was stupid to stop so close to the school's backyard, but I didn't say anything. I trusted Kelly.

I thin blonde girl opened the door a sliver. A second later the

69

door flung open, and she threw her arms around Kelly.

"Oh my God! Where have you been?!"

"I've been around." She pulled away and grabbed my arm. "This is my friend, Astrid. She looked at me, "Astrid, this is my friend, Tiffany."

Tiffany and I exchanged a "hi" and waved.

Kelly took Tiffany's hand, "Can we stay here tonight, please?"

"Yeah," she motioned for us to come in. "Dad's already passed out and mom's at work."

Kelly sighed, "Thank you so much!"

We followed Tiffany through the house. As we passed by the living room, I noticed her father in his chair, with his head back, snoring. Beer cans were lining the end table next to him. It was the familiar tableau.

Tiffany wasn't much for asking questions. She found us some pillows and blankets, and we made ourselves pallets on the floor. After all the running and adrenaline, Kelly and I were wiped out. We were out as soon as we put our heads on the pillows. However, it wasn't a restful sleep for me. I tossed and turned all night, plagued by nightmares.

I woke up just before dawn not feeling right. I tried to shake it off by focusing on plans for my new life, but I couldn't shake the malaise. Kelly noticed I wasn't right and gave me a questioning look. I waved her off, trying to convince myself as much as her that I was fine.

After breakfast, Kelly's friend pointed us in the direction of another wooded area that would take us to the edge of town. She also passed us a couple of bucks and a small bag of food. We hugged Tiffany and headed for the woods.

We walked a mile or so before we saw woods on the other side of the neighborhood. I'm not sure how long we walked before we came upon a small creek. Looking back on it, the whole thing was doomed from the start. Neither of us knew anything about survival. We figured if we stayed by the creek, we would be fine. I guess we were desperate enough that we convinced ourselves water would be a start and the rest would come.

But the next morning, Kelly and I knew I was sick. My brain

pounded against my skull, and I felt like I was on fire. I was fevered and clammy and the symptoms were enough to send us back to the school. It took us far longer to get back than it did to leave. I'm not sure how long it took, but when we got there, I wished I had died in the woods.

My father wasted no time getting to the school, and his stern face sent shivers down my spine. I nearly crumbled under his dangerous gaze. If it weren't for his friend Kevin, I would've hit the floor. My father said something, but between fear and fever, I don't know what it was. I do remember being put to bed and the nurse looking me over.

I vaguely remember the nurse suggesting I rest, but my father wouldn't hear of it. He figured if I were fit enough to get back to the school, I would be fine on the car ride back to Oklahoma. My heart nearly stopped. I didn't want to go anywhere with my father and Kevin. More than anything I didn't want to go back to that deranged circus my father called home. All I wanted was to be far away from all of them.

With my stomach churning, I tried to sit up. In my feeble

mind, I was going to make a break for it. The motion made the room spin, and I fell back onto the bed. Tears streamed out of the corners of my eyes. I just wanted to go somewhere safe.

Then, I heard a familiar voice. It took all of my energy to figure out to whom the voice belonged. Suddenly, it hit me. It was Meg, my brief roommate at the shelter. Meg was there with me.

Despite my foggy mind, I learned that Meg had reconciled with her family and went home. Apparently, I made an impression on her, and she looked me up. When she called my father's house, Lynda had told her their crazy story about my violent and thieving ways.

Luckily, Meg didn't buy that crap and talked her father into helping me. While she didn't know my story, she knew it wasn't a good one. She knew, just by the way my father acted at the shelter, that anything they said about me was probably a lie.

In fact, because of me, she realized most of her problems were nothing. They were the complaints of a spoiled child. She realized she had a loving home. Seeing my family's dysfunction helped her see that everything her parents said or did was done out of love. They just wanted what was best for her. So she wanted to repay me by sharing her home.

When my father got the call about me running away again, he let them know they could take me if they wanted. They confirmed they did and followed him to Kentucky. I cried and thanked them repeatedly. I didn't know the right words to express my gratitude.

Unfortunately, my father wanted me to ride back home with him and his friend. He wanted the opportunity to remind me of the rules. While I lay sick in the back seat, he reminded me of each rule with a punch or a slap to my head and body. All the while, his buddy was driving like nothing was going on. What it all boiled down to was, if you say anything against me, I will kill you. At the end of it I nodded, like I always did.

5

By the time I got to Meg's home. I was delirious from pain and fever. My father practically shoved me onto the curb. He dropped my bag next to me and left with Kevin. As always, without a backward glance.

I shyly peeked at Meg and her father, Jake, as they watched my father drive away. Their disdain for my father was obvious. While it was nice to have people on my side for once, I couldn't help but also feel embarrassed and ashamed. Whether I liked it or not, he was my father, and they not liking him felt like them not liking a part of me. I couldn't help but think, "join the club."

They helped me into the house, immediately putting me into bed. I sank into the plush bed with a lazy smile before passing out. I didn't leave that bed for the first week and a half I lived there. They didn't complain or berate me for being sick. Instead, they did whatever they could to make me comfortable and keep me entertained. I was cared for with love and attentiveness that I had never experienced before. It was a wonderful novelty to have people genuinely care about me.

They also cared about each other. In my household, Molly, Alice, and Lance were important. My father and stepmother took an interest in what they were doing and worried when they were ill. I was an afterthought unless they were angry or … whatever motivated them to abuse me. Seeing people living together, loving and encouraging each other was in sharp contrast to my upbringing. Growing up in a house where the people who should care about you don't, it's hard to imagine strangers being any better. Meg's family was amazing, and that scared me.

I had felt happiness before, and it didn't take long for it to dissolve into a torturous prison. Even with the calm, peaceful atmosphere, I couldn't completely relax. My body hummed with tension all the time, waiting for the other shoe to drop. I waited and waited and waited for it. Before I knew it, a month had passed, and no shoe dropped.

I had made it a whole month without being beaten, belittled, or raped. Jake, Meg and her mother, Marg, were as nice to me then as they had been when I was dropped off. It was a surreal dream come true. So slowly, as the weeks passed, my guard dropped. I stopped looking over my shoulder, waiting for something to happen. For the first time in my life, I started enjoying life.

Meg and I hung out day and night. We went swimming, biking, and hiking. We talked a lot too. Well, I let her talk about herself a lot. I didn't want to talk about my life before. She didn't need to hear all that crap. Honestly, I didn't want to think about it. It was much more fun to listen to her stories, and live vicariously through them. Thankfully, Meg understood and never pressed for anything more than I could give.

The year I spent with Meg's family was almost magical. I never wanted it to end, but in the back of my mind, I always knew it would. My father must have felt my happiness and ease and grew tired of it, because he showed up one Saturday morning.

The sight of him climbing out of a new truck made my stomach turn violently. I knew his visit was a bad sign. I ran to the bathroom as the doorbell rang. While I threw up, I could hear Jake opening the door, and giving my father a cold greeting. The conversation became hard to hear. For a moment, I thought my father might have left. I prayed I was right.

"I have a right to see her Jake! She's *my* daughter after all'."

"Yeah," Jake snorted, "You're a loving and dedicated father."

"What I am isn't any of your business. I don't give a damn what you think about me. That's my kid, and I want to see her!"

"Now Rich, she's been doing so good here. Just leave her here," Jake pleaded.

"No! Get her out here, and get her stuff packed. WE ARE LEAVING!"

Tears streamed down my cheeks. I knew it was too good to be

true. I knew they couldn't leave me alone forever. It was impossible for them. Leaving me alone would be like abandoning the game, giving up their power over me. This was the shoe I had been waiting for. When I finally looked into his eyes, I knew my life with Meg's family was just another part of the game. Now, he was bored and ready to move on to another part.

I numbly packed my bags. Meg helped me robotically. Nobody wanted me to go. In the time I had spent them, we had become a family. I finally understood what it meant to be part of a loving family. I was terrified of what the future held for me now.

My father watched me hug my adopted family with a smug smile. He tossed my things haphazardly into the back of the truck. I felt like a condemned prisoner heading for execution as he climbed into the truck. The only difference is a condemned man knows the end will come soon; mine was a harrowing mystery.

"You know I had to get them away from you." His eyes stayed on the road, "I know what he was doing to you. I couldn't let that go on."

My head spun toward him so fast my neck ached. "Jake never did anything to me!"

He snickered. "You know that's not the story you're going to tell, or at the very least, agreed to."

I crossed my arms. "I'm not lying about those people. They are the nicest, most generous people I've ever met."

Suddenly, we were on the shoulder of the road, and I couldn't breathe. It took a moment for my brain to catch up, but I realized my father's large, calloused hand was around my neck. I thrashed and pried at his hand as my vision grew spotty.

My father leaned into me; his hot breath reeked of stale beer. "You're going to do whatever I tell you to do, or else."

I could barely whimper at the "or else." He let go and shoved my head toward the door. Holding my throat, I gasped for air. I didn't need him to explain to me the "or else." I knew what he meant. He had threatened me enough times over the years. However, my father wouldn't let my imagination run wild.

"If you don't do what I say, I'll make you watch while I

torture your brother. If you try to look away, I'll cut off your eyelids. When I'm done with him, I'll kill you. Do. You. Understand. Me?"

Bile crept up my throat. I couldn't bear to watch my little brother suffer because of me. I wouldn't be able to live with myself, no matter how long my time would be. It wasn't an empty threat. My father always followed through with his threats. Shame washed over me as I nodded.

He waited for traffic and did a U-turn. "I'll take you back there, but you better leave by the end of the week. Get me!"

I wiped away a tear. It didn't make sense to me to bring me back, but I wouldn't question it. When we came back, I got out before the truck completely stopped. Grabbing my stuff, I ran back into the house.

Meg ran to me, swinging her arms around me, "You're back!"

"Yeah," I smiled tightly. "I convinced him to bring me back."

"Thank God," Jake said, pulling both of us into a bear hug.

My heart ached at the thought of leaving this behind. I tightened my hold on them and relished the feeling of love and acceptance. I truly loved being a part of this family, and I was going to miss it. I knew if I told them everything they would protect me as best they could, but I also knew my father would find a way to destroy them. I couldn't do that to them.

Three days later, I ran away. I didn't take much with me; just a couple changes of clothes and a picture of me and Meg. Wanted to leave a letter, but I thought it would be easier on them if I didn't give any explanations. I would rather them think of me as an ungrateful bitch and be safe than to know the truth.

I ran to the only other place I knew I would be safe - the youth shelter. Summer was scorching that year, and it took me all day to get there. I was exhausted, thirsty and ready to collapse when I saw Miss Ellen at the reception desk. It had been a while since I'd seen Miss Ellen, but she recognized me and immediately took me to a room.

She laid me down and left. Barely a minute later, she came back with a glass of water and a washrag.

"Astrid! My God honey, what happened to you?"

"It's a long story, Miss Ellen. Do you have room for me to stay?"

"Of course, I do." She smiled and dabbed my forehead with the wet cloth.

"Thank you," I whispered, dozing off.

I awoke a little while later, and Miss Ellen was still tending to me. "How are you feelin'?"

"A little better," I croaked.

"I think you have a touch of sun sickness." She pointed to a box fan sitting on a rolling cart. "I want you to drink plenty of water and rest in front of the fan for the rest of the day."

"Okay. Thank you, Miss Ellen."

Miss Ellen handed me a glass and stood. She had only taken a couple of steps toward the door when she turned around. "If there is anything I can do please let me know. I have resources to help you, Astrid. All you have to do is ask."

I nodded before taking a drink.

I knew she would help me if she could, but no one could help me. Between my father's military position, his best friend a cop, and my credibility shot, there was no helping me. I was stuck till my father was either bored with me or he finally killed me. Until then, I just wanted to keep others from getting hurt.

The kids in the shelter were not as friendly as before. I didn't hit it off with anyone this time. Instead, I spent most of my free time in my room reading. Books were a great escape. It allowed me to get out of my head for a while. Books also gave me a window into worlds that I couldn't imagine without them.

I had been at the shelter for a couple of weeks when Lynda showed up. It was her turn to stir the pot.

"Astrid, your stepmother is here to see you." Miss Ellen smiled wanly.

I cocked my eyebrow and marked my place in my book. "Did she say what she wanted?"

"No, but she doesn't seem happy to be here."

I followed her into the hall. "That makes two of us."

Miss Ellen snorted. "I put her in the meeting room."

We stopped at the door. Taking a deep breath, I glanced at her, silently asking if I had to do this. She hugged me. Her kindness gave me the strength to open the door.

The door had barely opened when Lynda said, "You're probably wondering why I'm here."

I nodded and then realized that was pointless because she wasn't looking at me. Her disdain for me was practically dripping off her. I took the closest chair to the door and focused my eyes on the off-white tiled floor.

"Yes," I murmured, crossing my arms.

"I'm ready to forgive you for all the trouble you put me through, and I want you to come home." Her tone was flat and condescending.

"Home?" I spat bitterly.

"Yes, home," She huffed. "You've been gone for the better part of two years, and it's time for you to come home."

I jumped up, my heart thumping frantically, "I don't want to go back!"

"It's not your choice, Astrid!" She sneered. "Truthfully, it's not mine either. Your father

wants you home. Forgiven are not,
I would rather you be anywhere
but there."

"No!"

"Yes! We are leaving today
whether you like it or not. Go
get your things, Astrid!" She
stood up menacingly slow, "I
would hate to have to punish you
on your first day home."

"I. Said. No!"

I bolted out of the room. Tears
burned my eyes as I ran past Miss
Ellen and out of the shelter. I
didn't care about getting my
things; I had to get out of
there. I couldn't go back to my
father's house. I had experienced
too much good to have to go back
to that house, back to that life.

I didn't have a plan. I had no
idea where to go. Part of me
wanted to go back to Meg's, but I
couldn't bring myself to do it. I
didn't want to have to explain
why I ran away. Then it occurred
to me to go to the college.

Halfway to campus, I heard a
police siren chirp behind me. My
heart sank, and I froze. I knew
who it was without turning
around. It was Kevin. He could be
either taking me home or into the
woods to shoot me. The way I
looked at it, if you like a man

like my father, you could be capable of anything.

The cruiser rolled into my vision, "Hi, Astrid! What's going on?"

I shaded my eyes to look over at him. "Hi, Mr. Steele. How are you, today?"

"I'm okay." He waved me over. "I got a call from the shelter that you ran off, and Miss Ellen was worried about you."

"I…" My eyes drifted to the ground. "I don't want to go home."

Kevin sighed, "Astrid if you don't go home, you're going to end up in a foster home. Do you want to be in a foster home?"

I peeked at him and shrugged. "Yes."

He gently lifted my chin, "Are you sure?"

I stepped away and squared my shoulders, "Absolutely."

With a sympathetic smile, he went around and opened the cruiser door. "Come on then."

I did get put into foster care. My first foster family, the Masons, were nice enough, but they knew my father. He would call or stop by a couple of times per week, reminding me to shut up and that I'm only alive because he wanted me to be. When he stopped by, the Masons would leave us alone to talk. That gave him an opportunity to remind me, physically, that he wasn't kidding. The Masons never looked at me hard enough to notice the bruises on my arms or the slightly swollen lip or cheek. Being at Mason's house was a lot like home, except my father had to travel farther to torment me.

I ran away after a little over a month. I took off in the middle of the night, headed for town. One of the best and worst things about living in a small town is everyone knowing everyone else's business. That's how I heard that an old school friend, Violet, was living with her boyfriend, Jack, in a trailer court on the outskirts of town.

Jack was the first bad guy I ever met outside of my father. He was a drunk and a drug addict. I had no idea what Violet saw in him; he didn't even have a pretty face. I was cautiously thankful that he let me stay with them.

Violet told Jack all about my dislike for home. She had also casually mentioned that my family had money. After a day and a night of drinking, Jack had convinced Violet and I that robbing them would be a great way to get back at them. Before I knew what was happening, I could come back with a sack full of my family's belongings.

My eyes were as wide as dinner plates when I saw everything emptied out on the coffee table. He had cash, jewelry, and various knick-knacks. I couldn't believe he had done it. Violet seemed less than surprised.

After a while, Jack grew restless. Every noise made him jump. Violet didn't seem bothered by his behavior, but it started making me nervous. To this day, I don't know what set him off, but he started threatening Violet with my father's penknife. I jumped in trying to calm everyone down. His cold eyes fell on me. He pointed the knife at me and threatened to cut me from ear to ear. Violet looked at me but refused to get involved. I ran out of the house and down the street like an Olympic sprinter.

I ran until I found a pay phone. Violet might not have been willing to help me, but I couldn't leave her there alone. I wouldn't be able to live with myself if he did something to hurt her. So I called the cops.

Part of me regretted that decision. Kevin, whether by fate or magic, was the responding officer. We all ended up in jail. I was arrested as an accessory to robbery and stayed in jail for several days. Since my parents were the victims, they didn't feel inclined to bail me out. During that time Kevin interviewed me several times. I think he believed I played a bigger role in the robbery than I did.

My father and stepmother eventually came down. They seemed to enjoy playing the forgiving victims and made a production out of how much he cared about me. I agreed to plead guilty and got a deferred sentence. Since they were the victims, we agreed to the transition period where we would stay in a rented home until they were sure I would be good. Then we could go back home.

The first week we spent at the rent house was the happiest I had seen my father since I was a small child. One morning I was getting cereal when my father came up behind me. My heart hammered at my ribs. His arms caged me against the counter.

"You have made me so proud," he whispered in my ear. "Between the running away and the jail time, no one will ever believe anything you say." He chuckled.

I said nothing. I wasn't going to feed into his disgusting euphoria. It didn't matter what I said or didn't say. Everyone in town knew our family was messed up, and they weren't doing anything about it. Besides, he was right. He wasn't just telling people I was a delinquent, now I was one.

He grabbed the back of my neck, squeezing it, "Did you hear me, Astrid?"

"Yes, Dad," I whimpered. "I'm a liar, and I have nowhere to go."

"Never forget, I am with you." He pushed my head forward and let go.

We stayed at the rent house for a month. After the first week, I stayed there mostly by myself. One bright side was being just around the corner from the college. Since I wasn't allowed in school, I spent much of my time at the college library reading. I cried when the transition period ended. Going back to that house meant I wouldn't be alone anymore.

6

Coming home was as miserable as I thought it would be. My father was still riding high on everything I had done to hurt my reputation. Lynda was as condescending as ever, but at least she was keeping her hands to herself. She was still living off her imagined benevolence for "forgiving" me my sins. My siblings, the people who I was willing to betray good people for, were indifferent to me being home. Once I was in the house, they went about their business. Sadly, it didn't bother me since I'd never felt close to them.

I was putting the last of my things away when my door opened. Instinctively, I jumped, bracing myself for an attack.

"Astrid," said a cold, gravelly voice, "It's nice to see you again."

It was Lynda's mother, Nancy. She grated my nerves. Nancy was the epitome of knowing something bad was going on, and doing nothing about it. She even told me to keep my mouth shut, so nobody thought poorly of her daughter or her choice of husband. Their reputations were more important than truth or justice for me.

Squeezing my eyes shut, I took a deep breath and plastered on a fake smile. "Nancy, how are you?"

"I'm doing well." Her tone was distant as she scanned my room.

"Good." I smiled tightly. "Thank you for coming to see me. I appreciate it." I nearly choked on those words.

"Well," she swiped at imaginary lint on her shoulder, "Lynda said it would be beneficial for everyone if we forgave you too."

My brows furrowed. "What did I do to you?"

Nancy stared at me like I was stupid, "For what you did to Lynda, of course, and for the stealing. Not to mention the things you told me about your father."

My lips curled in disgust. With everything Nancy had seen herself, I couldn't believe she would act like I was slandering a saint. My body was vibrating with rage. I squeezed the bedpost at the foot of the bed while I tried to calm myself.

"You mean when I told you about him raping?" I fumed.

Telling her was the stupidest thing I ever did. It was a moment of weakness after a particularly difficult night before. I thought, since she had kids and grandkids, she would help me. That was giving her more credit than she deserved. Instead of help, she made feel like I was spreading vicious gossip about my family.

She shook her finger at me, "I told you nothing good would happen if you persisted in telling stories."

Blood roared in my ears. It took every ounce of strength for me not to beat her like I did her daughter. What kind of people treat children, or anyone, like this – to mock them. Especially, when we both knew the truth.

My lip quivered, "Yes," I choked back tears, "I've learned my lesson. No one cares. I'm on my own."

We studied each other in my deathly silent bedroom. The tension was so thick; it was a living thing. My eyes grew colder the longer I looked at her. She finally turned to leave. I thought I saw pity flit across her face, or maybe it was guilt. Maybe it was just me imagining a small part of her cared. I'll never know.

My father wasted no time getting a beer once the in-laws left. The front door had barely clicked closed. I headed for my room, hoping to stay out of sight, out of mind. My father was a leisurely drinker. He would drink one right after the other until the beer was gone or he couldn't hold a can.

I sat stiffly on my bed with my forgotten book in my lap. <u>The Remains of the Day</u> was a good book, but I couldn't get comfortable enough to melt into the story. I knew something bad was brewing in the other room; I could feel the cold fury coming. I had a sixth sense for it.

The door burst open. I leaped
to my feet, the thud of my book
echoing in the room. My father
stood at the threshold, panting
and leaning on the door frame.
His eyes were flint; his face
contorted with antipathy.

I shook under his scrutiny. In
the time it took me to blink, he
had come across the room and
punched me. I landed on the bed,
nearly doing a backward
somersault. I was dazed; I wasn't
as conditioned to this as I used
to be. My father threw himself on
top of me. Sitting on my chest,
he rained down a mix of punches
and backhands. Everything was
happening so fast; it felt like
he had two extra hands.

Through it all, I tried to
fight back. One thing I learned
from my father was docility
didn't stop him. I wasn't going
to sit back and take it. I
managed to wrench one of my hands
from under his knee. I beat it
against his chest and scratched
at his face. Eventually, between
my squirming and his drunkenness,
I got away.

I nearly ran Lynda over as I
headed for the back door. I
didn't stop till I got to the
college. It was nearly nine when
I got there. Students were filing

out of the various buildings, giving me a chance to slip into one for the night.

Locking one of the stalls, I dropped the toilet lid and sat down. Somehow, some way, I had to get away from those people and stay away. I knew I could get by for a little while hiding on campus. I had spent enough time there to know where to go for food and where to hide.

So, for weeks, I spent my days in the library reading and my nights figuring out where to go from there. When I got hungry, I would go to one of the dorms and get something to eat. Their meals were set-up buffet style, so I acted like I belonged there. No one ever questioned me.

During that time, I met a freshman, Jane. She was a petite girl with long brown hair and large, kind eyes. I had seen here around as I made my rounds to all the dorms. One day she sat down next to me while I shoveled cereal into my mouth. She watched me with a knowing look. Jane was perceptive. Not only did she know I didn't belong there, but she also knew something was haunting me.

She picked at her food while she surreptitiously watched me. After a few more uncomfortable minutes, she cleared her throat. "What's your name?"

"Astrid," I replied around the cereal in my mouth.

She looked at me expectantly, "Astrid…?"

I glared at her suspiciously, "Just Astrid."

"Okay," she smiled tightly. "I like your name."

"Thanks."

There was another stretch of uncomfortable silence. I finished my cereal, but it was already souring in my stomach. I was sure she was going to bust me. While she pensively picked at her eyes, I was trying to figure out where I could go now.

"You know," her eyes casually drifted to me, "my roommate dropped out a couple of weeks ago. If you want, you can bunk with me."

My eyes narrowed, "What makes you think I need to bunk with you?"

She shrugged. "I don't know. You just look like someone that needs help. I want to help."

I crossed my arms, leaning back in the chair, "What's the catch?"

"There's no catch. I just want to help."

I eyeballed her for a minute, trying to figure out her angle. I had nothing. Even the clothes I was wearing were items thrown away or left in lost and found. She didn't seem to be one of those girls who had a thing for girls. I had nothing to lose.

"Okay," I nodded, "Thanks."

"Great," Jane beamed. "Let me show you our room."

Staying with Jane was the best decision. She was so nice and great company. I could tell she wanted to know what had sent me into hiding, but she never asked. I suppose she figured I would tell when I was ready. Perhaps I would have had I stayed with her longer.

I had only been living in the dorm a couple of weeks when my fledgling world fell apart. I was heading to the library when I caught a glimpse of an Army uniform out of the corner of my eye. My heart seized and froze. There was my father in full regalia, medals hanging proudly, talking to a scrawny, long-haired kid.

I came back to my senses and headed back to the dorm. Instead of going inside, I walked around to the back. It was no longer safe to stay on campus. The day had finally come for me to move on. I felt bad for taking off without saying goodbye. Jane had been so kind to me and deserved better treatment, but I had to put as much distance as possible between him and me.

I was back to square one. I had nowhere to go. The only future before me was the long stretch of road in front of me. Even though my future was uncertain, I took comfort that at least my future didn't involve my father or that family.

Along the back of the school was a neighborhood of older homes. They were from the late 1800s and in various stages of renovation. I was admiring the charm and character of the homes as I walked by. Then I saw a girl come out of one of the houses a couple of doors down. It was Rachel.

I used to go to school with Rachel. For a while, we lived in the same neighborhood. She was one of the few people who could testify to the craziness that went on at my house. I hoped she could help me.

I sprinted, waving my arms, "Rachel! I can't believe it's you!"

She turned around with her brows furrowed. Then, her eyes widened, and she smiled brightly. "Astrid! Oh my God, where have you been?!"

"Here and there," I hedged.

I caught a glimpse of a tall man coming out of the front door. Rachel turned her head and smiled at the handsome guy. He walked up to her, and she wrapped her arm around his.

"This is my cousin Brent," she beamed. "Brent this is my friend Astrid."

He held out his hand to me, "It's nice to meet you."

"You too," I smiled, shaking his hand.

We stood awkwardly smiling and looking at each other. I wrung my fingers, trying to decide how to ask Rachel to help me. Rachel noticed my nervousness and asked Brent to wait in the car.

Taking my hand, she guided me farther away from the car and whispered, "What's wrong?"

"I know it's been a while since I've seen you but," tears stung my eyes, "can you help me?"

"What you need?"

I shrugged, "Somewhere to stay or take me somewhere where I can stay. I've got to get out of this town."

She smiled wanly, "I don't know if there's anything I can do. I'd let you stay here if I could, but my parents wouldn't go for that. They would see it as getting in the middle of your family's problems."

"That's the story of my life," I snorted.

She gave me a piteous look. I could see her trying to figure out some way to help me. I knew it was a lot to ask, and I would be angry at her if she couldn't come up with anything. Just seeing her try meant a lot to me.

"Hold on a second," she squeezed my hand before heading to the car.

I scanned the neighborhood while I waited for her to come back. It was my attempt to look casual while others decided my fate. If Rachel and Brent couldn't help me, I would go over to the shelter and see if Miss

Ellen could hide me. Hopefully, Miss Ellen would know of a way to get me out of town.

"Astrid?" Said a deep voice behind me.

"Yeah?"

"Ummm," Brent shoved his hands in his pocket, "Rachel was just telling me that you needed to get out of town. She also gave me an idea of why you need to get out of town. I have an aunt that lives in Arkansas. I could take you over there you can stay with her for a while."

"You'd be willing to take me Arkansas," I asked, grinning.

"Yeah, I would. The only catch is you can have to tell people that you're 18."

"That's fine," I shrugged. "I'll tell anybody anything you want me to as long as you get me out of here."

He chuckled. "Well, all right."

"When can we leave?"

Brent gave a questioning look to Rachel. I could tell she was disappointed, but she smiled and nodded.

"We can go right now." He headed for the car.

I glanced guiltily at Rachel. "Are you sure? I'm sorry that I messed up your plans."

She wrapped her arms around me. "Yes I'm sure. We were just going to go screw around in Tulsa. Don't worry about it. I'm just happy that I found a way to help you."

"Thank you so much." I gave her a long squeeze, tears sliding down my cheeks. "I don't know how I can repay you."

She pulled away and looked me squarely in the eye, "Just stay away from that family of yours."

"Okay," I gave her a watery smile. "Thanks again."

I climbed into the car and headed toward an uncertain, yet certainly brighter future. I waved until Rachel disappeared from view. Once she was gone, I slipped down into the floorboard of the car to hide until we were out of town.

"Are you sure that's necessary?" Brent kept his eyes on the road.

"My father's best friend is a cop. I don't want to take any chances."

He shook his head, "Okay. I'll let you know when the coast is clear."

It wasn't long before Brent told me to sit back in the seat. The first half of the car ride was quiet. I couldn't believe I climbed into a car wit, a stranger, heading out of state. He seemed just as surprised by his offer to take me. Eventually, Brent broke the ice.

"So, like I said earlier," he glanced at me hesitantly. "I'm taking you to my aunt Betty's house. She's in her 50s, and she lives alone out in the sticks. She doesn't get a lot of company, so I think she'll appreciate you being there."

"Are you sure she'll take me in?"

"Yeah, especially if we tell her a little bit about why you left. She's got a kind heart. I think she'll understand and be willing to help you." He gave me a reassuring smile.

I gave him a small smile and looked out the passenger window. Brent's good looks made me shyer than usual. I felt like an idiot and a loser. He knew more about my problems than he did about me, yet I couldn't bring myself to talk to him.

It took almost two hours to get to his aunt's place just outside of Van Buren, Arkansas. It was a small two-story house at the end of a long driveway. The house was in a small clearing in the woods. Firewood was stacked neatly on the porch by the front door. The scene reminded me of a Norman Rockwell print.

Brent opened her door, "Wait here."

I nodded, watching him approach the house. The front door opened and a pretty dark-haired woman walked out. I couldn't hear them talking but judging from the hug and look on her face; she was very happy to see Brent.

I could see them talking. Every so often his eyes would drift toward me in the car. I couldn't tell by her facial expressions what she was thinking. Her smile never left her face, but it seemed to go up and down with each sentence Brent uttered. After several moments, I saw her nod and Brent giving me the thumbs up.

I got out of the car with my hands in my pocket. My face felt like I had sat too close to a fire. I was so ashamed and embarrassed to have to ask a complete stranger for help. I also felt grateful that there were people in the world willing to help a total stranger like me.

"Hi Astrid, my name is Betty." She held her arms out to me.

With a tight smile, I gave her an awkward hug. "It's very nice to meet you, Betty. Thank you so much for helping me."

"It's no problem, Astrid." She motioned for us to come into the house.

I had just passed the threshold when I noticed Brent did not follow. "Hey, Aunt Betty, I'm sorry to take off, but I got to get back home. Is there anything that you need before I leave?"

"Not today Brent. I'll give you a call if something comes up."

Brent waved at his aunt and looked at me. "You take care of yourself, Astrid. I'll be seeing you around from time to time."

"Thanks again Brent," I waved shyly.

Brent's aunt was incredibly kind. She was willing to share what little she had with me in exchange for my company and help around the house. In the time that I stayed with her, she took me to church and told me everything there was to know about her and her family. I answered some of the questions that she asked about my family, but I think she could tell it was hard for me.

Hearing so much about Betty and her family made me think about my own. I started to feel guilty about them not knowing where I was or if I was okay. I'm not sure why I felt guilty. My family was nothing like Brent and Betty's family. If my family had cared that much about me, they would not have abused me in the first place.

Weeks went by, and I couldn't shake that guilt. No matter what I told myself, I couldn't escape the guilt. So one day I made a collect call to my father's house. My stepmother answered and was elated by the sound of my voice.

"My God Astrid, where have you been?!"

"I've been staying with a friend's aunt in Arkansas."

"Arkansas!" She sounded amazed I'd gotten so far.

"Yeah, I just wanted to call let you know that I'm okay."

"Where can I pick you up at?"

My eyes narrowed, "What?"

"Where can I pick you up at in Arkansas? You need to come home." I arched my eyebrow at the tone of concern in her voice.

"I didn't call because I wanted to come home." I sighed, "I just wanted you guys to know I was okay."

"We're fine, but we want you to come home. Where are you?"

I don't know what came over me, but I told her where I was and how to get there. Within a couple of hours, Lynda and her father were picking me up from Betty's. I thanked her profusely for helping me. I was sad to be leaving. I didn't want to go, but I couldn't lie to Lynda either. My stupid guilty conscience shot me in the foot.

7

Once we got on the road, Lynda explained that had my father had been gone for several months on training. I thought that was odd since I had just seen Dad in town a couple of months back, but I didn't say anything. Lynda spent the whole car ride home talking about our family from her point of view. It was the calmest, most normal conversation Lynda and I had a long time.

She said she understood that she enabled my father to do the things he did. She said it was a lot easier to let him drink than to deal with the reason why was drinking. She knew the drinking caused other problems, but she was just as scared of him as I was. He was not the man she thought she married.

Lynda also took the time to apologize for how she treated me. She wasn't sure why she treated me the way she did. That was something she was still trying to work out. Either it was because she blamed me for the change in her marriage or his drinking brought out the worst in her. They both sounded like BS to me. Even at 15 I knew that you couldn't blame a child for an adult's problem.

"Your dad's been in AA since you left," Lynda smiled into the rearview mirror.

"Great," I nodded mechanically.

"We are both trying to make our home a better place for you kids. Running away like you did opened our eyes." She glanced over her shoulder at me.

I smiled tightly. Something was going on. Lynda was too nice. I didn't know what her angle was yet, but I was sure she had one. They had never done anything for me out of the kindness of their hearts; I couldn't imagine me running away could affect a change.

I waited every day for two months for things to go back to the way they were. Every time Lynda came into the kitchen while

I made myself cereal, I waited for her to hit me. I waited for her snide comments about my vomiting episodes. At the end of every day, I would scratch my head in amazement that nothing happened. I couldn't figure it out, was Lynda playing the game or were they serious about changing? Were crazy people able to change like that?

During that time, Lynda encouraged me to get in touch with my relatives in Illinois. I hated to admit it, but I did miss them. It was a perverse thought that stayed tucked in the back of my mind. It was like I wanted their love even though I knew I would never get it. I still wanted to try.

So one Saturday morning, Lynda and I sat down to call my Mom and sister. The call turned out just as I expected. My mother was more interested in talking to my stepmother than me. She did manage to give me half-hearted "hi" before our conversation dipped into awkward silence. I asked about talking to Grace, but she said Grace was too busy to talk to me. I knew my sister was in college now, so I understood and said maybe another time. My mother made sure I understood

Grace would never have time to talk to me.

I hung up the phone and shrugged, my lip quivering, "Well, I expected that."

Lynda put her hand over mine, "I'm sorry."

I slipped my hand out from under hers and shrugged again, "It's not your fault. It's the way she's always been to me. I'm used to it."

"Well," she picked up her address book, "Let's call your Grandpa."

I wiped away the single tear trickling down my cheek, nodding, "That would be great. It's been so long since I talked to him."

Lynda dialed the number and handed it to me as it started to ring. A shiver of excitement ran through me while I waited for him to pick up. He had always been kind to me, at least when no one else was looking. I didn't blame him for keeping his kindness a secret considering the harpies he married and spawned.

"Hello?" Said a deep and gravelly voice.

"Hi, Grandpa! It's me, Astrid! How are you?"

"What do you want?!" He snarled.

I felt myself paling at his harsh words. My hands shook as I handed the phone to Lynda who mirrored my pale complexion. Her expression moved from shocked to furious in the second, and she grabbed the phone from her hand.

"What is your problem, Mr. Barton?"

"I don't want that whore calling my house."

My stomach flipped violently at his accusation. Shame washed over me, welling my eyes. The walls felt like they were closing in, and it was getting harder to breathe. Where did my Grandpa get the idea I was a whore? How could he believe something like that?

"Who the hell told you that?!"

"Her dad told me all about it the last time he was up here visiting Grace." Lynda's eyes narrowed as she processed the news. "When was Rich up there? He never told me about a trip to Illinois."

"Just because he didn't tell you doesn't mean he didn't go." He sighed. "While he was here he told us Astrid started doing

115

drugs and working as a prostitute to feed her habit."

"And you believed him?" She cackled bitterly. "You know the kind of man Rich is. Why would you believe anything he said about her?!"

"I never had any problems with Rich. The problems between him and my daughter were their problems, and a lot of them were of her doing. Look I gotta go. I don't have time for this." The line went dead.

I sat there in stunned silence. Lynda watched me like she was waiting for something to happen. Maybe she thought I would explode in a furious rage at the revelation of what my father had told my grandfather. Strangely though, I didn't feel anything. If he had taken more of an interest in my life, it would hurt more. I couldn't lose what I didn't have. He was just one more person in a long line that hadn't cared about me.

Lynda was incensed. She hopped on a soapbox and sang praises about my father's honesty and trustworthiness. She was convinced Grandpa lied because my father would have told her he was going to go to Illinois. Besides, why wouldn't he take the rest of his family? His other kids would like to visit with her older sister. I said nothing the whole time; just shrugged and nodded while trying not to roll my eyes.

All the while, Brent stayed in the picture. He didn't understand why I came back, and I didn't either. We ended up agreeing it was what it was and he gave us an opportunity to hang out more. The budding crush I had on him the day he took me to Arkansas had cooled to friendship. He was kind, funny and made the days pass far more quickly than I would've liked.

The first time he stopped by the house was one of the most embarrassing experiences of my life. When Lynda opened the door and laid eyes on him, she became a giggly cougar. She fawned over him and touched his shoulders and arms like he was a fine cashmere sweater. It was almost comical to watch him go from flattered to freaked out in a matter of minutes. I quickly grabbed his arm and led him outside and away from her roving paws.

Brent refused to come to the door after that. Instead, I would come out when he honked. We hung out a lot at Rachel's house, but we did our fair share of fishing too. Brent was the first guy I had met who was nice. He never made me feel uncomfortable, and he never asked questions that he knew I wouldn't want to answer. Like others before him, he knew there was more to my story, but I would only tell it in my time.

The era of peace ended one Sunday afternoon when my father came home. I immediately stood as he walked in the door. I stood there rigidly as I watched him drop his bags wide-eyed at the sight of me. I braced myself as he came toward me, readying myself for the first blow. Instead, I was lifted and spun in a circle.

"Where the hell have you been?!" My father wrapped me in a bear hug.

I patted his back cautiously, "Arkansas."

He put me down and looked me squarely in the eye. "How did you get to Arkansas?"

Eyes drifted to the floor. "A friend of a friend took me."

"Well," he slapped my shoulder and grabbed his bags. "It's good to see you again. I've missed you so much, and I can't wait to tell you about all the changes I've made."

"Great," I absently rubbed my shoulder with a tight smile.

"Let me get my things unpacked, and we'll talk," he beamed and headed to his bedroom.

I sat back down on the couch. Between my Dad spinning me around the room and his happiness to see me, I felt a little dizzy. My father had not been this nice to me since I came home with him years before. I wanted to believe he could change, but after all the evil he did to me I didn't believe it. I couldn't believe it because if I did and he had not truly changed, it would kill me. Probably literally.

My father came back, and we had a long talk. He apologized for all the things he had said and done over the years. He admitted he had a rough childhood himself and didn't know how to be a father. Drinking helped him cope with his feelings of inadequacy as a father, as well as, some of his experiences during Vietnam. With a big sugary smile, he promised that things would be different and that he would be the father I deserve to have.

His confessions and promises pulled at my heartstrings. I wanted to believe him. I wanted to blame alcohol for all of the problems, but I couldn't. I couldn't let my guard down. My father was a seasoned hunter, and he knew that sometimes you have to wait out your prey. I was tired of being his prey. I accepted his apologies and told him exactly what he wanted to hear. I was back in survival mode.

Things stayed peaceful in the house. My father came home, ate dinner and helped the younger kids with their homework. It was a domestic side of my father I had never seen. Since I wasn't in school, I did most of the chores around the house. When I wasn't doing housework, I would hang out with Brent on his days off.

My father was extremely nice to Brent when they first met. Of course, I didn't tell him Brent was the one who took me to Arkansas. Some secrets can stay secrets. They shook hands and talked about sports. They were both Sooner fans, so that was one mark in the good book for Brent. Seeing my father with Brent made me wonder if he had changed. It was a dangerous thought that I couldn't keep from worming into my mind.

While I was gone, my father had bought a small trailer by the river. According to Lynda, it was his thinking spot. He used it as his base to fish and hunt. One day he asked Brent and I if we wanted to join him at the trailer for some fishing. The thought of going to the woods with my father made my skin prickle, but I didn't want him to think I was scared. Yes came out of my mouth before I knew what I was saying. Brent nodded his agreement, and we made plans to go fishing the next day.

Brent picked me up the next morning at 9 o'clock. We were supposed to meet my dad at 10; Brent wanted to leave early to make sure he was on time. We got to the trailer before 10 and found my father in a lawn chair, drunk. My stomach dropped at the sight of the beer cans littered on the ground around him. He had only been out since around 8 o'clock; he must have drunk one right after the other.

"You want to know a secret Astrid?" He slurred.

I glanced at Brent before cautiously replying, "Sure."

"I hate your stepmother," he laughed. "I've hated her since the year after we were married." He chugged the rest of the beer in his hand and tossed it. "She thinks that she knows everything. Everything! All she does is talk, talk, talk. She talks so much I've had fantasies about cutting out her tongue."

His eyes narrowed at Brent, "What's a life worth to you?"

"What?"

My father shook his head, "What is a life worth to you?"

Brent's eyes darted to me as if I had the answer to the question. I shrugged helplessly. There is no right or wrong answer with my father, but he expected an answer nevertheless. I pantomimed for him to say something.

"Umm… Li- Life is is ppppriceless."

"Are you sure about that?" He stood up.

"Y- Yes."

"Damn, I was hoping you would do me a favor," he sighed, grabbing another beer out of the cooler. He cracked it open, taking a long drink while he sat down. "Damn, I was really hoping you'd kill my wife. I'll make it worth your while. Once I get her insurance money, you can name your price."

Brent's eyes were nearly falling out of his head. His face was ashen, and his hands were shaking. I grabbed his hand, trying to reassure him that everything would be okay. Again, he looked at me for the answer, and I felt useless as I shrugged.

"I… I'm sssorry M-Mr. Clarke, but I can't do that."

He nodded casually and downed the rest of his beer. "FINE!" He took a deep breath, "That's fine."

I took a step back. My father had that familiar look in his eyes that made my blood run cold. His cold stare had fallen on Brent. He looked him up and down and then glanced over at me.

"You want to hear another secret Astrid?"

"Sure," I whispered, a tear ran down my cheek.

He leaned forward in the chair and whispered as if he were telling me a secret, "I don't like your friend Brent either."

I heard Brent gulp. My father smiled malevolently at the fear in Brent's eyes. "I'll be right back." He gave him a wink and smiled before heading into the trailer.

"Get out of here, NOW!" I kept my eyes on the trailer door.

"Come with me!" Brent tucked my arm.

I pulled away from him, but never took my eyes off the door. "No, I'll be fine," I lied. "Just get out of here!"

The sound of gravel crunching under his feet grew distant as he sprinted to his car. My father charged out of the trailer with a shotgun in his hand screaming, "WAIT!"

My heart seized. The first thing that popped into my head was "I knew this was too good to be true." I knew he couldn't change. It was all just another part of the game. He waved for Brent to come back. I didn't look at Brent when he came back. Fear and shame had frozen me in place.

My father waved him a little closer, a sinister smile playing on his lips. When he deemed him close enough, he tossed the shotgun at Brent. Brent caught it by the stock and barrel and stared at my father dumbfounded.

"What do you think of that?" He grabbed another beer from the cooler.

Brent glanced at it quickly and gave my father an awkward smile. "It's really nice."

"Yeah, it is," he smiled proudly. "I just bought that last week."

"Great," Brent chuckled nervously. He cautiously walked toward my father and handed back begun.

My father pulled his shirt off and took the gun with his covered hands. "Thanks."

My father took the gun back into the trailer. I grabbed Brent's hand and pulled him toward the car. "I think it's time for us to go."

We sprinted to the car and wasted no time getting out of there. Brent sprayed gravel everywhere when he punched the gas. I held on for dear life as the bumps and ruts in the road flung me everywhere. I could see my father in the side mirror waving goodbye like nothing crazy happened.

Brent said nothing on the way back to my house. I figured this would be the last time I saw him.

I couldn't blame him. Who would
willingly put themselves in
danger like that? If I had a
friend with a family as crazy as
mine, you wouldn't catch me
within a block of their house.
The tires squealed as Brent left
my house. Tears streamed down my
face as I waved goodbye.

8

After my father's spectacular fall off the wagon, everything went back to normal. My stepmother nit-picked and blamed me for everything in the house. When she grew tired of that, she hit me. All the while, my father would sit in his chair drinking beer until it was gone, or he was too drunk to hold the can. Now that I was older, when he came to my room, it was more often to beat me than rape me.

One day, a couple of weeks after the incident by the river, Brent knocked on my door. I opened it enough to slip out, quietly shutting up behind me. His jaw dropped. Then, a coldness took over him that I had never seen before.

"He hit you?"

I shook my head, "He's not the only one." Hugging myself, I took a seat on the top stair. "What are you doing here?"

He shrugged, "I wanted to see you. Maybe hang out?"

I touched my blackened eye and fat lip. "I'm not really in shape to be going out right now."

He sat next to me. "We don't have to actually go anywhere. I missed you. I missed talking to you."

I gave him a lopsided smile, "I missed you too."

Brent stood up, holding his hand out to me. "Let's go to the park down the road."

I grunted as I stood up and a shadow passed over Brent's face. "Let's go."

Brent and I spent hours talking about everything and nothing. Now that he had a taste of my family's particular brand of crazy, I told him more about my childhood. He sat in slack-jawed amazement that I was still alive. It also disturbed him that people knew about the abuse, and let it go on. I shrugged it off and tried to change the subject. My body hurt too much to climb on my soapbox.

The next thing I knew, a blinding white light was shining in my eyes. I squinted and shielded with my hand, trying to see beyond the light. Realizing it was a cop was bad enough, but realizing it was Kevin was worse. Kevin finding me means it wasn't by accident. My father had Kevin looking for me.

Suddenly, the strangest sensation came over me. My surroundings grew hazy like I was coming out of a dream. Something like a cord snapped in my mind, and I remembered something I didn't realize I had forgotten. There was another time Kevin was standing over me.

I was about ten. I don't know what I did to set my father off, but my father was punching me. Then he put me in a chokehold and dragged me to the bathroom. He pushed my head into the toilet. I tried to scream, but nothing came out. This assault was so much worse than anything I'd experienced before. I struggled against him and the water. Water rushed into my lungs, making them burn and feel heavy. My movements became slower until I slipped into nothingness.

I was floating. Below me, a man kneeled on the floor frantically trying to wake up a little girl. I had only a passing interest in the scene until I realized that little girl was *me*. Then I realized what had happened. My father killed me.

I remember feeling happy and relieved that I wouldn't have to suffer anymore. It was my first taste of freedom. I was ready to move on, but I couldn't go any higher. A disembodied voice told me it wasn't time yet; "He" was waiting for me. I had to wait for him. I didn't care about him; I didn't want to go back. The voice repeated, firmly, that it wasn't time.

The next thing I remember was looking up at Kevin, coughing up water. He scooped me off the bathroom floor and took me to my bedroom. His eyes were sad as he dressed me in my pajamas. I'd be sad too if I had a friend like my father. I'll never understand how he liked someone that he knew was a cruel deviant.

The haze dissipated as quickly as it came, or so I thought. When my vision cleared, I realized I was at the police station. My father's demand for answers resonated in the hall. I broke out in a cold sweat, and my heart thumped violently against my ribs. My body shivered with a fear that I had never felt before, because I remembered that my father had killed me before. All these years, I had feared the threat, but now I knew it was a promise.

The door flew open, slamming against the wall. "Let's go, Astrid!"

I cringed at the tone of his voice. I stood up, keeping my eyes on the floor. He grabbed my arm, digging his fingers into the muscle. "I should take you out tonight and kill you for embarrassing me, *again*."

The smell of stale beer invaded my nose. I turned my head, whimpering at the thought. Tears spilled down my cheeks. He yanked me through the station, while several officers watched. None of them cared. I was just another troublemaker. Don't bother to find out why a kid runs away from home repeatedly.

My father threw me against the truck, "Get in the car, now!"

I climbed in as fast as I could. It was a terrifying ride home. My father didn't say a word to me. He didn't even turn on the radio. I kept my eyes glued to the passenger window. I didn't dare look at him, especially now that I knew what he had done to me before. I prayed that if he did kill me tonight, he would make it quick.

He pulled into the driveway and headed into the house without saying a word. I slowly slipped out of the truck and followed him inside. The sound of a beer can opening echoed in the dark, silent house. I tiptoed to my room, closing the door as quietly as possible.

The next day was quiet. Lynda didn't have much to say to me other than my father would be gone for the day. I was relieved. The silent treatment from Lynda didn't bother me, but getting it from my father was unnerving. I quickly got around and took a book to read outside.

Brent came by in the afternoon to see how things went for me the night before.

I shrugged, "Dad yelled a lot at the station, but didn't say anything to me on the way home." I marked my place in the book. "I'm not sure if that's a good thing or not. What happened to you?"

His eyes widened, and he blew out his breath. "They checked me for drugs and alcohol. When they didn't find anything, and I wasn't drunk, they told me not to sleep in the park again."

I shook my head. "If it were anyone besides Kevin, we wouldn't have been taken to the station. The cop would have just told us to go home."

Brent chuckled, "Yeah, you're probably right."

The rumbling of an engine in the distance caught my attention. My father was almost home. Brent noticed my body stiffening. He looked around, trying to see what distressed me.

"I hear my Dad's truck."

"Oh." He stood up, putting distance between us.

My father gave us an offhanded wave as he parked in the driveway. He hopped out of the truck with a smile. His smile was too friendly, and he was far too chipper to be the same man that scared me last night. I glanced at Brent before looking back at my father.

"Astrid, we're going over to Lynda's mom and dad's tonight to play cards." He looked at Brent, "You're more than welcome to come along if you like."

"Umm… sure. Thank you, Mr. Clarke."

"Great! We're going to leave in about an hour." He nodded and headed into the house.

"Cards?" His eyebrows drew together.

"They like to play cards together. It's been a long time since I've been there." I shivered at the memories.

Brent sat back down, "What do they play?"

I shrugged, "A little of everything. It just depends on what everyone feels like playing. Sometimes it's poker; sometimes it's canasta."

Brent and I stayed outside until it was time to go. He offered to give me a ride, and I gladly accepted. When we arrived, I introduced Brent to everyone. Nancy seemed pleased that I had brought my friend over. Lynda, however, seemed angry about it. I put it out of my mind, hoping we could have a normal evening.

The first couple of hours were great. We were all having a good time playing Crazy Eights. It was fun watching everyone teach Brent how to play. The game was going well until Lynda looked over at

Brent and me, laughing as I explained a rule to him.

"You know Astrid, you don't have to date that asshole if you don't want to."

My smile dropped from my face, "We're not dating." I shrugged, glancing at her. "I'm not dating anyone."

My father threw his cards down. "There's no reason to lie to us, Astrid. I'm so sick of your lies and drama." He flipped the table over.

I jumped away, heading for the door. Halfway there something pelted me in the back of my head. It hurt but didn't stop me. I was almost out the door when something hit me in the head again. It was heavier than the last object and made me stumble on the porch. I scrambled to my feet in time for something else to hit me in the back, making me tumble down the steps.

Brent, my tall, muscular friend, whizzed past me, heading for his car. He'd had enough of the craziness. It hurt that he left me like this, but I didn't have time to mourn as my father descended on me, raining punches all over me.

Lynda grabbed his arm at one point, trying to stop him. He jerked his arm away and started kicking me. Her mom and dad got in the middle, pulling him off me enough to get up. Gathering everything I had, I sprinted to the bar owned by Lynda's parents across the street.

I burst in, blood running from my nose and the back of my head. A couple of burly men leaped to their feet to help me. My father wasn't far behind me. Just as the men got to me, I felt a hand wrench my head back by my hair. Hair ripped out, but I hardly felt it over the throbbing.

He continued to pull me back to the house by my hair. The burly men followed us out, yelling at him to leave me alone. He shouted for them to mind their own business and pulled on me harder. For once, someone decided to do the right thing and call the cops. I heard the sirens in the distance. I prayed Kevin wouldn't be one of the responding officers.

Unfortunately, Kevin was one of four officers that responded. My father threw me to the ground and waved at them.

"Hi, Rich," Kevin tipped his hat, "What's going on this evening?"

"She's at it *again*." He shrugged, combing his fingers through his hair. "I just don't know what to do."

Kevin and his regular partner, whatever, nodded while the other officer narrowed his eyes. "What exactly did she do that would warrant a beating like that?"

Kevin held up his hand, signaling for the new guy to shut up. "She's a prostitute."

He tilted his head, processing that information. "Okay, but that still doesn't explain why he's beating her like this."

Kevin pointed at my father, "That's his daughter, and that's all you need to know. Go back to the car; we'll handle this from here."

The new guys gave me a sympathetic smile and went back to his cruiser. Shaking my head, I stood up. I was tired; tired of my evil family, and tired of the willfully blind people in town. I wanted to get out of there and never come back.

"I'll leave her to you Rich," Kevin said quietly.

Spitting out a mouthful of blood, I shouted, "It'd be nice if, for once, you would protect and *serve* someone other than my Dad."

I saw a bright light before I felt or heard my father's hand hit my face. I stumbled but stayed on my feet. Nancy wrapped her arm around me, guiding me toward the house.

"One of these days you'll learn to keep your fat mouth shut," my father bellowed.

"He's right, Astrid," Nancy whispered. "You do need to learn when to stay quiet."

She sat me down in the bathroom and pulled out her first aid kit.

"He's evil." I sobbed.

"I know he is, but that doesn't change the fact you need to stop provoking him." She lifted my chin, looking me in the eyes, "Do you want him to kill you?"

I pulled away and shook my head.

Nancy started cleaning and bandaging my wounds. With each cut she cleaned, her expression softened more. Deep down inside, I think she did feel sorry for me. It was unfortunate she didn't feel sorry enough to help me.

"Shoot!" She looked through her medicine cabinet. "It looks like I'm out of gauze. I'm going to check the other bathroom. I'll be right back."

I waited until I heard her rifling through the drawers to sneak out the back door. I sprinted into the woods, heading for the intersecting highway a mile or so up the road. Then I followed that highway just inside the treeline. I hoped to hitchhike to the next town, but after nine o'clock, that stretch of road became nearly deserted.

I had walked for about twenty minutes or so when I saw headlights going my way. Once I knew the truck didn't belong to anyone I knew, I ran to the road, waving my arms around. The truck rolled to a stop.

An older woman, with kind eyes, rolled down her window. "What happened to you?"

"My father beat me up," I panted. "Can you please take me somewhere, anywhere?"

The woman looked at her husband. He looked me up and down with a grim look on his face and nodded. She opened her door and scooted to the middle of the bench.

"Thank you so much. I really appreciate it." Tears streamed out of my good eye.

"Think nothing of it." She patted my hand.

"Where are we going?"

"We're going to take you home, and help you get better. Once you're healed, we'll help you figure it out from there." She gently touched my swollen eye. "What's your name?"

"I'm sorry. It's Astrid." I held out my hand, "What's yours?"

She took it gently, "I'm Ally, and that's my husband, Jeremy."

"It's nice to meet you both."

They lived on the outskirts of the other side of town. Ally told me they were retired and had a small hobby farm. I could tell she wanted to know what had happened to me, but she didn't want to ask right away. Considering how bad I felt, I had to look worse. I couldn't expect her to take me in without some explanation.

When we got to her house, she took me into the bathroom. She finished what Nancy had started while I told her the story. Her disdain for my family practically oozed out of her. She was familiar with my father and stepmother through her friend, who was a neighbor of theirs.

I had stayed with them for about a week when Ally sat down at the kitchen table while I ate breakfast. Despite not liking my family, she thought it was important for me to let them know I was okay. I wanted to argue with her, but I couldn't bear to after the kindness she had shown me.

The phone picked up on the first ring, "Hello?"

"Hi, it's Astrid." I curled the phone cord around my finger.

"Where are you at?"

"I'm staying with some nice people just outside of town."

"Okay," his tone was cold and unfeeling, "I talked to my brother in Kentucky, and he'd like you to come out there for a while."

"Is that uncle Tyler?"

"Yeah. Can your nice people meet me at the grocery store? I'd like to get you to him today." My mouth opened and closed before I put down the receiver to talk to Ally.

I explained the situation to her. She nodded, taking my hand and squeezing it. "It's probably for the best you stay with your kinfolk. Maybe they'll be better than your family. If it doesn't work out, though, feel free to come back. You're more than welcome. I'll get ready to take you to town."

"I hope so," I snorted, "They couldn't possibly be worse."

I sighed, picking up the receiver. "I'll be at the store in a half-hour or so."

He said okay, and the line went dead.

I gently touched the back of my head, near the crown. It was still sore from last weekend, but I didn't lose as much hair as I thought. I dreaded the ride to Kentucky with my father's chilly mood. Mostly because I wasn't sure I would make it to Kentucky.

9

Uncle Tyler was a shorter version of my father. I could tell right away; he wasn't any different than my father. The look he gave me when I got out of the truck wasn't the type an uncle gives to his niece. His wife, Mandy, noticed as well, but instead of being appalled at him, she glared at me. There's not a sane person to be found in my family tree.

For the days that I was there, my uncle was sickeningly nice to me. It wasn't the kindness of an uncle to his niece, but of a seducer to his victim. My skin crawled every time I looked at him, so I tried to avoid him as much as possible. His wife, on the other hand, became more hostile as each day passed.

It all quickly came to a head one night at the bar where Mandy took me. She was already half lit when we got there, but she bellied up to the bar asking for a shot and a beer. I watched her grow drunker and drunker while I tried to figure out why she took me there in the first place.

When she started talking, loudly, about her husband's predilections, it became clear. Instead of seeing me as a child her husband wants to victimize, she saw me as a rival for her husband's affections. I tried to assure that I wanted nothing to do with them like that, but she refused to believe me. She told me that if I ever even look at him again, she was going to cut me up into little pieces.

I didn't know what to say to her, so I sat there jaw dropped and eyes wide. The bartender overheard her and was appalled. She waited until I got up to go to the bathroom to offer me a place to stay with her. Her offer caught me off guard, but it didn't stop me from saying yes. So my new friend, Jean, put my aunt in a taxi and took me home with her.

Jean was a nice lady, but she didn't have much. She lived in a small apartment on the rougher side of town. I knew I couldn't stay there long, but it would give me enough time to call Ally and get home. Ally didn't have the money to get me a bus ticket right away, but would get it worked out.

Unfortunately, it took her more time than I had to scrape the money together. Somehow my father had found me. He was furious that I wasn't staying with his brother anymore. Explaining the situation would've been useless, so I kept my mouth shut. Instead of taking me home, he took me down to the police station.

It wasn't until after I was booked I found out what he had told the police about me. He had spun the same yarn about attacking my aunt with a knife. I'll never figure out how they managed to make those charges stick, but they did. I ended up going to a juvenile detention center for nearly four months. I used to think of the boarding school as a prison, but it was nothing compared to that place.

I had only been there a couple of days when one of the girls attacked me because I looked like a girl with whom her boyfriend had cheated. I tried to tell her in between punches that I had nothing to do with her boyfriend; I didn't even know who he was. She couldn't hear me through her rage, so I fought back. By the time the guards pulled us apart, we both looked equally worse for wear. That fight gave me enough street cred for other people to leave me alone.

From there, they bounced me around from halfway house to halfway house until my last court date. After all those months in jail and halfway houses, they dropped the charges for lack of evidence. It was another part of my father's game. He sent me there to prove to me that he could make my life a living hell. So uncle Tyler took me from the courthouse directly to the bus station and sent me home.

When I got off at the Muskogee stop, there was no one waiting for me. I called Ally collect to see if she could come pick me up. I stayed with Ally for a couple of months before DHS got wind of it. Since my family had moved without a forwarding address, they placed me in foster care.

My foster parents, Jim and Bernita, were an older couple who had raised their own children and decided to help less fortunate

kids. They were kind and generous
people who gave me the sense of
family I had missed for so long.
Two other foster kids were
staying with them that were close
to me in age, Matt and Natalie.
It took us a while to warm up to
each other, but soon Natalie and
I were friends.

One hot June day, Natalie asked
me if I wanted to go to a party
with her. Of course I did. I
rarely got a chance to go to a
party. So we spent most of the
day picking up perfect outfits
and primping ourselves. I don't
know why I took so much care with
how I looked, but I knew I had to
look my best.

As soon as I laid my eyes on
him, my heart was gone. He was
gorgeous with dark eyes and hair.
When his eyes met mine, I could
tell he felt it too. I knew deep
down in my soul that he was the
"he" I had been waiting for. It
was all I could do not to run and
jump into his arms.

"Hey," I tugged on Natalie's
sleeve, "Who's that guy over
there?" I pointed to him.

She smiled. "The guy with the
white ballcap and chew in his
mouth?"

"Yeah. Yeah. That's him. What is his name?" I vibrated with excitement.

"That's David." She giggled at the dopey look on my face. "If you'd like I'll take you over to meet him."

I blushed, "Could you?"

"Sure," she said, then paused. "But I won't have to." She pointed his direction.

He was coming toward us. My excitement crumbled into anxiety. He was the first guy I had ever liked as more than a friend. I didn't know what to say to him. Seeing my distress, Natalie grabbed my hand, squeezing it.

"You going to be fine. Dave is a really nice guy. Just be yourself, okay?"

"Be myself. Be myself. Okay." I nodded, plastering on a big smile.

"Hi," his eyes shifted shyly. "I'm David Mayhue." He held his hand out.

I took it, hoping my voice would work. "I'm Astrid Clarke."

His smile widened, "It's nice to meet you."

From that night on, David and I were inseparable. If he wasn't working, and we weren't sleeping, we would go to the movies, hang out at the bathtub rocks, or hang around my house. He made me laugh, and see the world through less jaded eyes.

I never had much to say when we talked about our families. I didn't want to lie to him, but I also didn't want him to know how damaged I was. So I would either change the subject or give short, generic answers. Since I lived in a foster home, he knew my story was probably not a good one, so he didn't press.

With each caress of my cheek, kiss on my lips, and a warm hug, my brain believed what my heart already knew; he was it for me. He was my reward for surviving my journey from one side of hell to the other. I was as perfect for him as he was for me.

I've never thought of our relationship as a whirlwind, but maybe for a 16- and 17-year-old it was. David and I had only been together for a few months when I found that I was pregnant. Seeing a positive pregnancy test didn't bother me in the least. I knew everything was going to be okay because I was with David. He would stand by me no matter what.

We made a date to go to the bathtub rocks. It was one of my favorite places to go. There was something magical about it. I also wanted David to take me there because I didn't want him to suspect anything. I spent the whole week before on cloud nine. I was ready for this next step in my life.

It was warmer than usual for November. The smell of rain hung in the air while we soaked our feet in one of the natural pools. We held hands, and talked about nothing. When it came time to tell him the news, I found myself tongue-tied. I wasn't scared to tell him, but I didn't know how to tell him. I didn't just want to blurt it out. I wanted to make telling him special.

"David," I cuddled his arm with a huge smile, "I found out some amazing news earlier this week."

"Really?" He kissed my head. "What did you hear?"

I turned my head, put my chin on his shoulder. I wanted to look into his eyes when I told him. "We're having a baby."

His eyes searched mine, "Having a baby?"

I nodded, not trusting my voice.

"Oh my God!" He grinned, and enveloped me in a bear hug. "A baby!"

I snuggled his shoulder. "A baby," I whispered, choking back tears.

He pulled away quickly and looked me in the eyes. "The only way this night could be better is if you agree to marry me. Will you marry me?"

"Yes!" I sobbed, "yes I'll marry you."

We got married a couple of weeks later at the Justice of the Peace. It was a small, informal wedding. I never allowed myself to dream about my wedding day because I wasn't sure I would live long enough to have one. When the time came to plan my wedding, I figured out I didn't care about how the wedding happened, I just cared about who I was marrying.

By the time December rolled around, I was married to the man of my dreams with a baby on the way. Christmas had come early for me. I was the happiest I'd ever been in my whole life. Somehow I found a great guy, and I was starting a family. It was my light at the end of the tunnel.

His family was also wonderful. They took me into the family without any awkwardness. He made me feel like I'd always been there. David's mother was especially supportive to me throughout my pregnancy. I rollercoasted between excitement and depression the whole time. I worried that I wouldn't be a good mother because I had so little experience with good mothering. During those low points, she would wrap her arms around me with a reassuring smile and say, 'Don't worry Astrid, I'll be there to help you.'

10

For the next 25 years, aside from the normal obstacles, I loved my life. I had two great kids, and a husband I was in love with more than the day I married him. We went through our fair share of feasts and famines, but none of that mattered to me because we always had a loving household.

However, my spells of vomiting never ceased. I grew up thinking it was from all the stress of living at home, but when it didn't stop after I got married, I wondered if there was more to it. I went to countless doctors looking for an answer, but they always came up empty handed.

The answer came one night after I was rushed to the hospital. It was a particularly bad episode.

My stomach burned and ached for a few days, and I couldn't keep anything down. The pain and nausea made it difficult to sleep. I was lucky if I got a couple of hours a night. I drank Mylanta and Pepto-Bismol, trying desperately to calm my stomach. Then I started throwing up blood. It wasn't the first time I had thrown up blood, but I had never thrown up so much.

David wasted no time getting me to the hospital, and for once I didn't argue. I was just as scared as he was. I doubled over in the seat partially from the pain and partially because I was cold. I also started getting drowsy. David frantically tried to keep me awake, asking me all kinds of questions. I don't remember anything after we pulled up to the ER entrance.

The next several days passed in a blur of pain, vomiting, and vital checks. My sleep was plagued by vicious nightmares that made me flail and scream. It wasn't until the haze passed that I realized those nightmares were not merely dreams, but memories. They were memories of things my father had done to me years before that my mind stuffed away. Then it clicked. I've been trying to remember these things for years.

The doctor explained that repressed memories are a way for your mind to protect you from things you can't process. While that made sense to me, I didn't understand why it picked some events and not others. I also didn't understand what was triggering these memories. He didn't have any answers for me because the mind was still a mysterious thing. All he could suggest was to see a therapist.

It would be a while before I could make an appointment with a therapist. I spent several days in the hospital while they got my ulcerative colitis under control and gave me a couple of blood transfusions. Even with sleep medicine, I still wasn't getting restful sleep. I was weak and exhausted.

When they release me from the hospital, I was prescribed bed rest for a while. I decided to use that time to write about my life. If I couldn't get to a therapist, then pen and paper would be my therapy. So as I lay in bed, healing from my illness, I poured out all the things I remembered about growing up.

Some people repress memories because they can't deal with the fact that something horrific happened to them. For whatever reason, my brain had decided some of it wasn't so bad, and some of it was. What's strange is that some of the memories I repressed weren't nearly as bad as some of the memories that I didn't. There was no rhyme or reason to it.

Time went by and I got stronger, not just physically, but mentally as well. Bleeding out all that poison from my past on to those pages was a weight lifted off my shoulders. It felt good getting it out. The journaling also helped me get a better idea of what triggered my sickness. When I was young, I got sick because of fear and shame. Had I had a constant source of support and protection, I might not have gotten sick.

I figured out that I got sick now not because I was scared for myself, but because I was fearful of what my father would do to the people I love. He was never one to make idle threats. My father is the embodiment of evil, and he makes no apologies for it. Even when his health was uncertain, he never apologized for the years of torment. He wasn't sorry.

Journaling helped me come to terms with the fact that, despite everything, I still love my mother and father. They were worthless as parents, but they did give me life, and I have found joy in that life. Ultimately, the beginnings of this book have helped me lay the foundation for my healing.

I'm a couple of years into my recovery since that time. My illness is under control and I enjoy time with my kids and grandkids. Memories still come back to me from time to time. Anything can trigger them; a smell, a phrase, even something as basic as getting up in the morning. Thanks to my family and the program I'm in, I'm able to absorb these memories instead of letting them tear me apart.

Now I'm strong enough to take the awful things that happened to me, and use them to help others, specifically to help kids. Even as a child, I didn't believe that I deserved what happened to me. I didn't deserve the beatings. I didn't deserve the ridicule. I didn't deserve it from *anyone*, but especially not my family. Growing up the way I did, I saw a lot of other kids in a similar boat. Some were broken beyond repair by a cruel family, and a system that got there too late.

With my children grown, David and I decided to become foster parents. We wanted to give a loving home to kids that might not know what that means. I'm hoping, with my experience, I can help kids reach beyond their broken homes to aspire for a better life because they've experienced it.

When a child speaks up about abuse, please listen. Be the person they can depend on to defend them.

About the Author

Jennifer Neugin is a wife and mother of two living in northeastern Oklahoma. She enjoys reading, volunteering, and spending time with her family. Jennifer and her husband are also foster parents and enjoy helping children find stability and strength. This is Jennifer's first book.

Printed in Great Britain
by Amazon

38661002R00094